nightmare academy

Frank Peretti

nightmare academy

THE VERITAS PROJECT VOLUME 2

THOMAS NELSON
Since 1798

NASHVILLE   DALLAS   MEXICO CITY   RIO DE JANEIRO   BEIJING

Published in Nashville, Tennessee, by Thomas Nelson. Thomas Nelson is a registered trademark of Thomas Nelson, Inc.

Thomas Nelson, Inc., titles may be purchased in bulk for educational, business, fund-raising, or sales promotional use. For information, please e-mail SpecialMarkets@ThomasNelson.com.

Unless otherwise noted, Scripture quotations used in this book are from the King James Version of the Bible (KJV).

Library of Congress Cataloging-in-Publication Data

Peretti, Frank E.
    Nightmare Academy / Frank Peretti.
       p. cm. — (The Veritas Project ; v. 2)
    Summary: Elijah and his sister Elisha go undercover to investigate a mysterious school that is sheltering runaway teenagers for a sinister purpose.
    ISBN 0-8499-7617-0
    ISBN 1-4003-0340-0 (Trade Paper)
    ISBN 978-1-59554-446-9 (repackage)
    [1. Schools—Fiction. 2. Runaways—Fiction. 3. Christian life—Fiction. 4. Mystery and detective stories.] I. Title. II. Series.

PZ7.P4254 Ni 2002
[Fic]—dc21

2002070060

Printed in the United States of America

08 09 10 11 12 QW 5 4 3 2

To Barbara Jean, my love, as we continue our wondrous journey together.

1

the kid in the
padded room

His mind told him, *insisted,* that he was running, putting one tattered, bleeding foot in front of the other—even though the ground did not move under his feet, turned when he did not, or inclined steeply upward though he saw no slope before him. He closed his eyes, but he could still see. He screamed, but he heard nothing. The pathway became a precipice and he tumbled headlong, falling through space. He was under water. He tried to swim; suddenly his groping arms were pulling him forward through hot, dry sand. The sky above was red like a sunset, the earth below an eye-buzzing purple—then green, then gray, then red as the sky turned green.

Where he was, or why, or when, or who, or how, he could not know, could never know.

There were no days, no hours, no moments, no way of knowing, no chance for knowing how long he'd been here.

Been where?

No place, at no particular time.

He was once a fifteen-year-old boy, cocky and wayward. He once had a brother, a sister, a father and mother. He had a name, a house, a school, and a life—and he thought he knew something. Maybe he thought he knew it all.

But that boy, and that time, and that life had become . . . nothing. Non-things.

There was no fifteen-year-old boy here. No knowledge, no thought, no reason. There was nothing here but terror, endlessly repeating cycles of it, layer upon layer of it—with more, more, more to come, in swirling, kaleidoscoping sounds, images, and sensations, pulsing, pounding, surging, throbbing like a swollen thumb.

The only reality.

He stopped, fell against a gnarled old tree. . . .

The tree toppled unnaturally, crumpling like a wad of paper, without sound. He fell. . . .

And hit the ground. Cold ground. Grass. Stones. They didn't move, didn't change. The earth was motionless under his body, the dew of the night cold and soaking through.

The tree he thought he would lean on, that had fallen . . . was a metal door, now slowly closing behind him, creaking on its hinges.

Without a thought, he was on his feet, running away. He could see nothing in the dark, was not aware of the branches and limbs striking against him, was not aware of the aching in his chest, the pounding of his heart, the gasping for air.

He just ran.

Nelson Farmer was tall, with a long horse face and a worried look that just stayed there, even when he wasn't worried. Right now he *was* worried, making his face sag to new depths of sourness.

"Harborview," said the taxi driver, pulling up in front of an immense hospital in Seattle.

Harborview Hospital, part of the Seattle skyline for generations, was known as the place to send the really tough cases. Victims of accidents could be helped in any good hospital; victims of *horrible* accidents were sent here, as were the burn victims, abuse victims, disaster victims, and . . .

Farmer didn't have a label for the victim he was hoping to find here. He might have a name, but at this point he couldn't be sure. He would know in the next few minutes.

Dr. Cal Madison, white-haired, balding, and soft-spoken, met him in Observation and Evaluation. "Thank you for coming, Mr. . . ." He looked once again at Farmer's business card. "Farmer. My! From the D.C. office! You've come a long way."

"Not really," said Farmer. "I was out on the West Coast on business anyway. I just made a little side trip."

Madison moved through the front office and into a narrow hallway. Farmer followed.

"I expected the Bureau would just send a local person," Madison commented.

"This could be a special case," Farmer replied. "The local office may not have the records on this one yet."

"Hmm." Madison had to think about that one. "Anyway, I'm not sure what information you have at this point. . . ."

"He was found on the highway, somewhere in Idaho?"

"North Central Idaho, I think. A very mountainous region, not much civilization to speak of."

They entered a darkened room with one large window. The window, of two-way glass, opened on another room. That room was roughly ten feet square, softly lit, and the walls and floor were covered with thick, quilted padding. Against the far wall was a very simple, low-built cot, also heavily padded; in the center of the room, curled up on the floor like a cowering animal, was a boy. He was clothed in hospital pajamas and lay motionless except for a trembling, involuntary curling and uncurling of his fingers. His eyes stared at the floor, unwavering, unblinking.

Dr. Madison explained, "We judge him to be about fifteen years old. We've had to dress him because he can't dress himself. He wasn't carrying any ID, so we have no idea who he is."

"And I suppose he can't tell you?"

"You need to see this," Madison said, slipping out the door. He closed the door behind him, leaving Farmer in the darkened room. A moment later the door to the padded room opened, and Madison stepped inside. He knelt beside the boy and asked him, "How are you doing?"

> His eyes stared at the floor, unwavering, unblinking.

"I don't know," the boy replied in a low monotone.

"Do you need anything?"

"I don't know."

Madison looked toward the two-way glass as he asked the boy, "Can you tell me your name?"

"I don't know."

Farmer could hear everything through a small intercom speaker beside the window. As Madison asked the boy a few more questions and the boy replied "I don't know" to every one, Farmer pulled a file folder from his briefcase and opened it. The first page included a photograph of a young man.

The very same young man.

Farmer held the photograph at eye level, letting his gaze shift from it to the face he saw through the glass. There was no doubt.

He closed the folder, put it back in his briefcase, and snapped the briefcase shut.

When Madison returned, Farmer shook his head, looking impressed. "Very disturbing."

"It's as if his whole mind has been erased," said Madison, still marveling. "All knowledge, all logic . . . gone."

Farmer nodded thoughtfully. "I'm glad you called. I'll arrange to have him transferred immediately."

Madison appeared puzzled. "Excuse me?"

"The best way for us to identify this young man and return him to his parents—if there are any—is to put him under protective custody so we can make a positive identification."

"I'm not familiar with this procedure."

"We don't use it very often, only in special cases such as this one. It'll take me a little while to arrange for a car and for a suitable room—"

"No, no, wait. I'm sorry. That's impossible."

Farmer tilted his head, raised an eyebrow. "Come again?"

Madison's face was etched with disbelief and a little indignity. "This young man is a patient in this hospital, and we can't release him."

Farmer's spine stiffened visibly. "Dr. Madison, the Bureau for Missing Children has its procedures, and I'm afraid—"

"No. Absolutely not. He's in no condition to be moved anywhere. He's malnourished and underweight, he can't clothe himself, he can't feed himself, he can't—"

"Need I remind you with whom you're dealing?"

Farmer's words struck Madison wrong, very wrong. "Perhaps I should confirm that information one more time."

Farmer glared at him a moment, then produced his card again.

Dr. Madison read it again: Nelson Farmer, Field Investigator, Bureau for Missing Children, Washington, D.C.

Farmer followed his card with an official, laminated photo ID from the office in Washington. "Would you like to see my driver's license? I also have a firearm permit if you'd like to see that."

Dr. Madison handed back the photo ID and shook his head. "It won't change anything, anyway."

Now Farmer raised his voice. "I beg your pardon?"

Dr. Madison replied in his same businesslike tone, "When this boy's *parents* say to release him, then I'll release him. Until then, he's under my care, he's my responsibility, and he stays here."

"We don't even know who the parents are."

"Well, that's your job, isn't it, to reunite missing and runaway children with their families? Now, we've provided the boy's likeness, his fingerprints, and everything we know about him. You're the one with the nationwide computer database. I think it's time you got to work."

Farmer grabbed up his briefcase. "This is not going to go well for you."

"I'll see you—and your threats—to the door, Mr. Farmer."

A week later, Dr. Cal Madison attended a medical conference within comfortable driving distance from Washington, D.C., where he arranged to have dinner with an old friend.

Now they were sitting in a secluded booth—a table Madison had asked for specifically—enjoying a fine meal and formal surroundings. Dr. Madison spoke in secretive tones, carefully pausing whenever a waitress walked by.

"I had my secretary go to BMC's Web site, and within an hour she had a positive identification of our patient." He handed the documents across the dinner table to his guest. "Alvin Rogers, age fifteen, Thousand Oaks, California. He and a friend, Harold Carlson, ran away a month ago. The Carlson boy is still missing."

"So now you're wondering why this Farmer character needed custody of your patient in order to identify him?"

"Exactly. It wasn't necessary. I called the BMC, and he works for them, all right, but the people I talked to weren't aware of any such policy. Farmer said he came by because he was already on the West Coast anyway, but according to the people at the central office right here in Washington, he left rather urgently, with only one destination, and that was Seattle."

"Hmm."

"There's more. When I expressed my surprise that the Bureau would send one of their top-level people clear across the country instead of letting the local office in Seattle handle it, he told me the local office probably didn't have the records yet. Do you find that believable?"

"You got the information right off the Internet. If you could get the information, then certainly the branch offices would have it."

"So we're clear on that."

"Oh, yes."

Madison allowed himself a quick sip of water. "And, incidentally, I never heard back from Farmer. Maybe it's because we found the boy's parents ourselves."

The guest looked up from the documents with raised eyebrows. "Oh, you did, really?"

"He and a friend, Harold Carlson, ran away a month ago. The Carlson boy is still missing."

"It couldn't have been more simple. We got their name and phone number from the Web site, gave them a call, and they flew up from California the next day."

"Well, good enough."

Madison broke into a smile, perhaps his first smile of the evening. "When Alvin saw his parents, heard their voices, and just got a loving hug, it made a world of difference. He came out of his stupor almost immediately. He was able to feed himself. He asked for some real clothes and dressed himself. It was beautiful."

"So I suppose you've sent him home?"

"Eh . . ." Madison sadly wagged his head. "He came out of his stupor, yes, but his mind is badly scrambled. He's afraid of being left alone, and he has trouble sleeping. We've tried to find out what happened to him and where he was for a whole month, but all we can get out of him is a stream of nonsense—ramblings about nothing being real, gravity turned upside down, time running backward, all sheer lunacy—and someplace he keeps referring to as Nightmare Academy."

The guest repeated the words to be sure he'd heard them correctly. "Nightmare Academy?"

Madison nodded. "It frightens him to talk about it—enough to make me wonder whether it might be, at least in some sense, real."

The guest stroked his brow, staring at the half-eaten steak on his plate. "Not a lot to go on."

"But enough, perhaps, to interest you and Veritas? I'm very concerned, especially for the other boy who's still out there somewhere, and what about the other missing children and runaways? Whatever happened to Alvin Rogers could happen to them."

The guest, a man named Morgan, paged through the documents one more time, thoughts racing behind his inquisitive, brown eyes. "I'll put some feelers out. I'll let you know, hopefully by tomorrow."

In Washington, D.C., far from the Capitol dome, was an old, red-brick office building with office space and apartments for rent. Morgan, middle-aged, bald, and bespectacled, arrived early, eager and anxious, almost forgetting to grab the morning paper before he went into a plain little office on the fifth floor. The small black letters on the office door quietly announced: The Veritas Project.

He was the first one here. Consuela, his secretary, was no doubt en route, as was Carrie, the office assistant. He flipped the light switch on without having to look at it and strode quickly to the fax machine.

A fax had arrived. From the letterhead, he knew it was the one he was expecting:

The White House.

Excellent. The president had received his message from last night and was responding.

But . . . strange. The president didn't usually send faxes to this office on White House letterhead. Usually, the message came on plain, white paper, no fancy labels, no obvious identifiers, nothing to call attention—

He froze momentarily as his eyes fell on the message:

UNDER NO CIRCUMSTANCES ARE YOU TO INVESTIGATE THIS

Morgan stood there a moment, the fax in his hand, seeing in his mind that big white residence half a city away.

This *was* from the president, wasn't it? The sender's number at the top of the page was correct, but this response was anything but typical. By prior agreement, the president did have a voice in which cases Veritas would take and which it would refer elsewhere. But the president had never sent such a short message, and never in all-capital letters, and never without any explanation or follow-up questions—or at least some kind of guidance on how to answer back.

Morgan took the fax into his office, tossed it onto his cluttered desk, and sank into his chair, letting it swivel him toward the window. Staring at a dismal segment of the Washington skyline, he debated whether he should just call the White House, but decided against it.

The front door rattled open. It was Consuela. "Good morning, boss."

"Good morning," he half muttered, trying to think.

She paused to stare at him with her large, Latin eyes. "Is there trouble?"

"Maybe." He thought a bit. "Yes."

"I'll make the coffee."

"Please."

"Oh!" She came into his office. "You left your paper by the fax machine."

She brought him the morning paper he'd forgotten about, unfolded it, and—

An envelope fell to the floor.

"Oops," she said.

Morgan stared at it for a split second, then stooped down, picked it up, and carefully opened it as Consuela watched.

Inside, he found a DVD in a white, windowed envelope. A small note was attached, bearing only two words: CALL THEM.

"Consuela," he said, an incisive glint in his eye, "call the airlines, book me a flight for Missoula, Montana."

She sprang for her desk.

Morgan pulled out the materials he'd gotten from his dinner with Madison and thumbed through them once again. "The Springfields need to see this one firsthand."

With his finely toned muscles straining and sweat on his brow, young Elias swung the iron door shut and dropped the bolt into place as the rest of his family scrambled about the lab in search of anything they could use to barricade the door.

The beast was coming down the hallway. They could feel the pounding of his footsteps shaking the floor.

Elias's sister Lisa brought a chair. As she brushed her long blond hair from her face, Elias could see that fear filled her eyes. Even so, she was still beautiful.

Elias took the chair and braced it against the door. "Thanks."

She answered, "I'm not doing this for you."

"So you're still angry?"

"This is all your fault! You should have selected a better brain!"

Elias was offended. "I selected the best brain money can buy. It's highly intelligent, highly rational! That beast can solve the most complicated equations in mere seconds!"

"But it doesn't care about people!"

"Who cares? Besides, I'm not interested in your notions of *should*. I did what I thought was right."

"But you were wrong."

"In your opinion!"

Just then, their parents came with a large table, and all four of them leaned the table on end against the door.

BOOM! BOOM! The sudden pounding told them where the monster was at: just outside the door, trying to smash it open.

"This is all your fault! You should have selected a better brain!"

Norton, the father, marveled. "What intelligence! What power! We've created a magnificent new creature!"

Susan, the mother, looked at him in horror and anger. "A magnificent new creature? Norton, we've created something evil and now there's no controlling it!"

He sneered at her even as they braced their backs against the door to keep it shut. "Evil? Come now, my darling! Since when have you adopted such old, antiquated notions? Good and Evil are only an invention of our society, a matter of opinion."

"But that thing wants to kill us!"

"Well . . ."

"And that's evil!"

He thought it over even as the door thudded against his back with each impact of the beast's angry fists. "Well, I can't say it's evil, but I'm not comfortable about it."

"Neither am I," said Lisa, helping to hold the door shut. "Perhaps we should have given the beast a, a *conscience*."

They all looked at her as if she were mad.

"Based on what? Feelings?" Elias shouted.

"Self-interest?" Norton fumed.

"Oh, he has that!" Susan sneered.

"Well, morals then."

"Morals?" Elias scoffed.

"Whose morals?" Susan snorted. "We went through all that, remember? We couldn't decide."

"We had no right to decide!" Norton objected. "We can't impose morality on something we created. We can't impose right and wrong on anything! There is no truth! What a monster believes is true, is true for him."

BOOM! BOOM! BOOM! The door and the barricade were weakening.

"So here we are," said Susan.

"No," said Lisa, backing away from the door. "Here you are. You made the creature, you can live with it—or die with it. I'm getting out of here!" She ran for the stairway on the other side of the lab, the stairway that would lead to the outside, and freedom.

"Hey," Elias yelled angrily, "you were involved in this project just as much as we were!"

"In your opinion!" she called back.

"But you aligned all the joints and synchronized the cardiovascular system! You, you even sewed his outfit!"

"That was then. This is now!" With that, she ran up the stairs, through the outside door, and away, leaving them behind.

CRACK! GROAN! The door was coming apart.

"I, I just can't stand it any longer!" Susan cried, moving away from the door.

"Susan!" Norton shouted desperately. "Susan, don't go! Stand with me! Help me!"

> **BOOM! BOOM! BOOM! The door and the barricade were weakening.**

She kept backing away, shaking her head. "No, Norton, no. There are too many things more important to me. Our house. Our money. The Gladiola Society. I was going to have my eyes lasered. I can't miss all that!"

"But I need you!"

"Oh, Norton, you're resilient, you'll recover, you'll see! I just need to find my own path—such as, out of here."

"But, but you can't do that!"

She looked at him quizzically. "I can't? Who are you to tell me I can't?"

"If this monster gets loose, he'll terrorize all mankind!"

"I suppose you see something wrong with that?"

Norton had to think about it. "Well . . . I can't say there's anything wrong with it—but I'd feel uncomfortable about it."

"Well, those are your feelings." She headed for the stairs.

CRUNCH! The table barricade was bending like weak cardboard. The door was breaking open.

"Susan!" Norton screamed.

As Susan ran up the stairs, leaving them behind, Elias admitted, "She has to do what's right for her." He stepped away from the door. "And so do I."

"Not you, too!" Norton exclaimed.

Elias was backing away quickly as pieces of plaster and fragments of doorframe began to fall around him. "It's been fun, Dad, working on a family project together, creating a whole new breed of man. But I think Lisa may have had a point. We gave our guy incredible strength and terrific brainpower, but you know, a sense of right and wrong would've been a good idea—even if there is no such thing."

"Son! Don't leave me here alone to face this monster!"

"Well Dad, I would stay, really, but it's starting to get uncomfortable. I'm not happy here anymore."

"Son!"

"Besides, who's to say there's really a monster crashing in here? Maybe that's just a matter of opinion, too."

A rivet bounced off Norton's head as he marveled at such a thought. "Opinion? You call this a matter of opinion?"

"Can't call it a matter of truth, now can I?" Elias headed for the stairs. "Looks like a nice day outside. Of course, that's only a matter of opinion."

"Son, have you no honor?"

Elias stopped to think about that. "Well, I really don't like running out on you like this, but I can't say it's wrong." And with that, he was up the stairs and gone.

Norton knew it was useless to resist. He dashed away from the door and turned to see the iron door flex, warp, and give way with a crash.

The monster, towering and mighty, entered the room, looking about for helpless human flesh to devour. The huge red eyes immediately focused on Norton, who was shaking with fear, but resolute. The thing took one step forward.

"Stop!" Norton yelled. "I command you to stop!"

The monster raised an eyebrow. "Are you talking to me?"

"Yes!" Norton replied. "I am your master! You have to do as I say."

The monster was obviously amused. "This is a joke, right? Me, do as you say? Take a look, buddy. I'm stronger than you. I'm bigger than you. End of discussion."

The monster, drooling hungrily, moved forward. . . .

2

on the darkside

And that, unfortunately, was the end of Norton,"
Nate Springfield read aloud, smiling at the strange similarity his daughter's characters bore to a real family—theirs. He looked up from the manuscript. "Norton?"

His sixteen-year-old daughter, Elisha, blond and pretty, grinned sheepishly across the dining table. "Well . . ."

"I mean, your mother, Sarah, gets to be Susan, Elijah gets to be Elias, you get to be Lisa—but *Norton?*"

"It's the first name I thought of that started with an *N.* I can change it."

Nate waved that aside. "No, Norton's fine. I'm resilient. I can recover."

"So what do you think?"

Nate deliberately took a long pause, cleaning his reading glasses, stretching his big frame a bit, checking the weather out the window. He leafed through his daughter's writing assignment again, page by page. This was Elisha's last home school assignment for the year, and she was late turning it in. Now, as a matter of discipline, she had to finish it before she could go horseback riding with her brother. And Nate, a former Montana lawman who used to "wait" confessions out of suspects, thought a little anxiety would do his daughter good. "Mm. You split an infinitive here."

She looked where her father was pointing. "But Dad, that's in a quote. The character doesn't have perfect English."

"I notice that character's your brother."

Elisha squirmed but grinned. "No. He's Elias. Fictional character. Elias." She was quick to add, "But I said he had finely toned muscles!"

Nate tried to stifle a laugh but could only stifle half of it. "Okay, I'll give you that." He went to the next page. "Huh, what's this? The sudden pounding told them where the monster was at . . ."

Even Elisha was horrified to see the sentence in her own writing. "I can't believe I did that."

"It's not in a quote this time, sweetheart."

Elisha was mortified. "No. It sure isn't."

"Never put where and at . . . ," he began and she joined in unison with her father, "in the same sentence."

"So what should it be?"

She made the correction even as she said it. "The sudden pounding told them where the monster *was.*"

"Very good."

Nate laid the pages down on the table in front of him and leaned back. "So tell me. What does the monster represent?"

Elisha was disappointed. "You don't get it?"

Nate smiled. "I want you to tell me."

She twisted her mouth in thought, then answered boldly, "Mankind without truth, without God-given morals. He has strength, he can think, he can even feel things emotionally—but if he isn't given a good, solid standard for right and wrong, then there's nothing to keep him from using strength and reason and feelings in selfish ways, even destructive ways."

"So, on the one hand, we tell ourselves that none of us are subject to any moral law outside of ourselves, and then we wonder . . . ," Nate prompted.

"We wonder why people do such evil things, why there's so much violence in the world, why people rob and cheat and betray each other. But when we erase truth from our thinking and say there's no right or wrong except for what each person thinks is right or wrong, well, we get the kind of world we deserve."

"And who ends up making the rules when we reject truth?"

Elisha adopted a grim, guttural voice. "The biggest, meanest, toughest dude." She used her own voice to add, "Whoever has the most power—the biggest army, the most money, the most votes, the most newspapers or television networks. When there's no truth that applies to everyone, then there's no way to argue for the rightness or wrongness of anything, and when that happens, whoever has the most power calls the shots."

"Like a monster running amok."

She brightened. Her father got the point. "Right."

Nate nodded, quite satisfied. "Well done, Elisha. Very well done." She grinned from ear to ear. "And now, I'm sure your brother would like to get some riding in before the day's gone."

"Yes!" Elisha exclaimed, jumping up, hugging her father, grabbing her cowboy hat, and heading for the door.

"Don't slam the screen—"

The screen door shut with a bang.

Elijah Springfield, Elisha's twin—the one with the "finely toned muscles"—had saddled the horses. His own steed, a chestnut named Charlie, stood patiently, oh so patiently, in the center of the Springfields' big barn, waiting for Elijah to make still another attempt at an experiment. Holding a long rope suspended from a ceiling beam, Elijah stood atop a towering stack of hay bales, staring, thinking, and staring again at the straw-strewn floor of the barn, then at the high, post-and-beam walls surrounding him, then at the ceiling beam to which the rope was secured, and then at his horse—still standing obediently, but only for so long.

The big question: Launching from this location, would he have enough inertia to kick off from the north wall, swing over to the west wall, swing in a downward spiral, and finally return to where Charlie was waiting at the very limit of the rope's decaying swing, thus coming into contact with the saddle while in a state of near weightlessness? If Charlie felt nothing, and mostly, if Elijah felt nothing, then his prediction based on the available data would be correct and the experiment would be a success—not a Nobel prize winner, but a success. He could see the trajectory in his head, as clearly as if he'd drawn it on his eye's view of the barn with bright yellow chalk.

Ready.

He gripped the rope tightly, checked the diagram in his mind one last time, and then started with a quick run off the hay bales.

He was flying, suspended, the north wall approaching, the rope moaning against the beam.

BAM! His feet hit the wall, his legs flexing like springs, and he bounded off like a billiard ball. Perfect angle.

He was lower now. The arc of the swing was decaying, but that was all in the plan. The west wall was coming at him.

BAM! Second rebound successful. *I should work for NASA.*

Now, one last spiral down, coming back toward his starting point, but below it now, right along the base of the hay bales, and there was Charlie's hind end, like the planet Earth from a spacecraft window, and just above it, the saddle, ready for a soft landing . . .

The approach of a leg-kicking, blue-jeaned, leather-brimmed spacecraft spooked planet Earth, and he trotted out the barn door

He was flying, suspended,
the north wall approaching,
the rope moaning against the beam.

just as Elijah reached the last, dying inch of the rope's swing, that minuscule moment of weightlessness when a landing would have been perfect. . . .

With a cry of frustration and despair, he clung to the rope as it carried him backward. He let go and fell into a pile of soft straw carefully placed there—in case something went wrong. By this time, although he hadn't mastered a weightless landing in a saddle, he had become quite skilled at landing in straw when something went wrong. He rolled into it, head over heels, half disappearing under the swishing stuff, the world going dark as his cool leather hat with the rattlesnake band scrunched down over his eyes.

With an angry growl he sat upright, brushing the straw off his arms and shoulders. "Charlie! You keep throwing variables into the equation!" He lifted his brim, letting the daylight back in. "If you'd only spook at a uniform rate—"

There stood his sister, weight shifted to one hip, hat cocked back on her head, watching him with great amusement.

"Hey, Einstein, let's do some riding."

"It's about time, Hemingway!"

She gave him a hand up. "So let's go, before something else stops us."

They hurried out of the barn. Charlie and Pardner, saddled and ready, awaited them by the fence. The afternoon sun was still high and the Montana sky deep blue. There would be time to ride the ridge behind the ranch, and maybe even get as far as the tree line where they'd spotted bear tracks just two days ago. Elijah mounted Charlie in quite the conventional way—Charlie didn't mind *that*. Elisha put her foot in the stirrup—

And the dinner bell rang. Not for dinner. This was a special ring, calling them to the house for something important. Elisha, her hand on the saddle horn, wilted, and then let go. "I hope it's you this time!"

Elijah dismounted, slightly miffed. "Hey, I turned in my paper yesterday, and I fixed that fence rail! I owe no man anything!"

They came around the barn and looked across the pasture toward the big log ranch house. A rental car was parked in front, and Mom and Dad stood on the veranda with . . .

Was that Mr. Morgan?

They gathered in the lofty, rough-hewn family room—Nate and Sarah Springfield, Elijah and Elisha, and the rarely seen Mr. Morgan—settling into the couch and chairs and on the big stone hearth while Morgan showed them photographs, documents, and other information he and his little Washington staff had gathered. Then he slipped a DVD into their home entertainment system.

"The clips you're about to see were videotaped at Harborview Hospital in Seattle by a friend of mine, Dr. Madison. I sent this footage to the White House along with our proposal, and you've seen the response I got: Under no circumstances were we to investigate this. Then lo and behold, within minutes, I found the entire contents of the videotape copied onto this DVD and hidden between the pages of my morning newspaper, along with a handwritten note."

The Springfields looked at each other.

"I don't get it," said Elisha.

"Believable denial," said Nate.

"Exactly," said Morgan. "If anything goes wrong, if the wrong people find out about this, the president can always say he told us not to get involved, that his administration had nothing to do with our investigation. Whoever sent the DVD did so without the president's direct knowledge, and he can say so."

"Sounds shady to me," said Elisha.

"It is. But it's obvious this whole operation has to be conducted with the same kind of caution, in the utmost secrecy."

"Why?" Elijah asked.

"I don't know," Morgan replied. "That's the rub. You're being asked to find out some things without knowing entirely why, or who knows why, or why such information is so important to . . . whomever."

Sarah, in her gardening clothes, her blond hair tied in a scarf, shrugged her shoulders and said, "Sounds like a government project to me."

"Believable denial," said Nate.

"It does indeed."

"So let's see what's on the disk," Nate said.

Morgan pressed a button on the remote control and the wide-screen television came to life. Upon seeing the very first image, the Springfields leaned forward in their seats, eyes riveted to the screen.

They were watching the mindless, blank-eyed behavior of Alvin Rogers. He was in hospital pajamas, standing in the center of the padded room and twitching nervously, looking at nothing, as a hospital nurse tried to start a conversation.

"Can you raise your arms for me?"

"I don't know."

"Don't you want to put on a fresh shirt?"

"I don't know."

"We'll get you changed, and then you can have some lunch. Would you like that?"

"I don't know."

The recording played on for several minutes, showing the nurse feeding him, Dr. Madison examining him, a therapist exercising him, and all of them trying to get through to the boy, trying to get him to acknowledge knowing something, knowing *anything*.

They all failed.

"He sounds like a skeptical philosopher," Elisha cracked. They all looked at her strangely, so she tried to explain. "You know: the ones who say nothing is true, that truth doesn't exist. If truth doesn't exist, then you can't know anything."

"Watch what happens next," said Morgan.

A man and a woman entered the padded room, and the kid, crazy or not, fell into their arms and started crying.

"He knows who Mom and Dad are," said Sarah, getting a tear in her eye.

"So he knows *something*," said Nate.

"And immediately he started talking," said Morgan, "but check this out."

The recording cut to a later scene. Now the kid, frightened and agitated, was spilling a torrent of words to his folks as they sat on the floor beside his bed. "I, I come to see the sky, but it was upside down. And I run, but not swimming, just, you know, running, and climbing . . . scratch myself. It was dark, too, hurt my eyes."

"Could you wind that back?" Elijah asked.

"Don't worry," said Morgan, "there's more just like it."

The kid kept going. "Terrible. Terrible. I kept falling, going up, never stopped and it hurt and I just didn't know."

"Where was this?" his father asked.

"Bending down, couldn't reach it . . . couldn't climb, either . . . had to go swimming . . . but the door wasn't there."

His father said to someone off-camera, "Where in the world has he been? Who did this to him?"

Morgan interjected, "Listen to this."

"Nightmare," said Alvin Rogers.

Alvin's mother asked, "What?"

"Nightmare." The boy began to tremble. "Nightmare Academy."

His eyes grew wide as if looking into a hell only he could see—and no more words came, only a long, pitiful wail. He began to kick and struggle, trying to back away from whatever he was seeing.

"Turn . . . turn the camera off," said his father while trying to hold the boy down.

The image shook, then blinked out.

Morgan pressed the stop button. "One month before this was recorded, Alvin Rogers was a fairly normal high school sophomore in Thousand Oaks, California. He was bright, did well in math and science, and stayed out of trouble. For whatever reason, maybe just for something crazy to do, he and a friend named Harold Carlson ran away from home and got as far as Seattle before disappearing altogether. Now Alvin has turned up crazy and Harold is still missing. I guess you can figure out what your assignment is going to be, if you want it."

"Find out what happened to Alvin," Nate responded.

"And what became of Harold," Sarah added.

"And what the Nightmare Academy is," Elijah said.

"And what the truth is behind the whole thing," Elisha concluded.

Morgan nodded. "We'll put you in touch with a youth shelter in Seattle where the boys were last seen, and see if you can pick up their trail from there. I'll help you in any way I can, but remember, we're hunting for something that cannot know it's being hunted or it might disappear before we can find it."

"And we don't even know what it is," Elijah said. "Cool."

Nate leafed through the documents spread out on the coffee

table, reviewing each one and passing it along to the others. "We're going to have a lot to discuss."

"Guess I'd better unsaddle the horses," Elisha said, a hint of disappointment in her voice.

Seattle, Washington, is a beautiful city at night—a blanket of jewels mirrored in water—and when the sky is clear, the glimmering towers of downtown mingle with the stars.

But like every city, Seattle has its darkside—its troubled streets, its districts of decay that become gathering places for those who have nowhere else to go. In the cold glare of the streetlights, in the shadows of the alleys, the homeless, the lost, the destitute, and the runaways walk up and down the blocks, hands in pockets, eyes downward. They are lonely, but afraid of strangers, without shelter and hoping to find a lonely curb, porch, landing, or doorway to call their own for the night. Sometimes they cluster with other wanderers, either for company or simply because there is only one place available out of the rain.

This night, two wanderers apparently found each other while trying to stake a claim to a small stretch of concrete sidewalk and marble building that were still warm from the daytime sun. One was a boy about sixteen, dressed in ragged jeans, stocking cap, and tattered, oversized mackinaw. The other was a girl about the same age, with black, stringy hair, wearing a khaki jacket, jeans with holes in the knees, and a second-hand wool cap. Her only luxury was a pair of headphones, apparently her way of shutting out the outside world. They spoke little, but curled up against the exhaust-blackened marble of the old publishing firm, trying to share the same precious piece of ground without getting too close or too friendly.

Across the street and up half a block, in the doorway of a bygone brewery, a tired old vagrant relaxed on the concrete steps, his back against the bricks, just watching the never-stopping traffic. He coughed, pulled the collar of his old coat closer around his face, and spoke in a quiet voice, "Are you warm enough?"

Down the street, the girl heard the question through her headphones and called softly to the boy, "Dad wants to know if we're warm enough."

"Plenty," said the boy.

"We're fine," she spoke to the air.

"Fine and bored," the boy added. "Except for that panhandler, we haven't found anyone to talk to. Things were better last night."

"Do you think we should try somewhere else?" Elisha asked.

The vagrant spoke into his collar, "How does it look to you, Sarah?"

At the other end of the block, in the back of a large van, Sarah sat before an impressive bench of electronic gear and radio receivers, monitoring the conversation, a headset to her ear. "We might try under the overpass again. The people at the youth shelter say a lot of runaway kids congregate there on the weekends after it gets late."

Elisha passed the word along.

Elijah looked at his watch. "It's 11:07 and 40 seconds."

Elisha smiled. Her brother was proud of his extremely accurate watch. "I think it's getting late."

Nate responded, "Are you kids ready for another night under the overpass?"

Elisha made a face despite herself. "Working on it." She told her brother, "They're talking about another night under the overpass."

"Well, hopefully we'll meet a different bunch," Elijah offered, "somebody who might know something."

"It's just hard to—Whoa, just a minute. Somebody's coming."

Elijah tried to look without looking. He saw her, too. "I think she's looking at us."

While Elijah and Elisha acted indifferent and preoccupied, Nate could see the woman they were referring to. She was a young and pretty redhead, and obviously not a runaway or vagrant; she was dressed casually, but dressed well in dark slacks, woolly red sweater, light jacket, and pricey running shoes.

"She's looking at us, all right," Elisha reported.

"Hi," said the woman, and Nate and Sarah could hear her voice over their kids' radios.

"Hi," Elisha responded in the dull tone of a glum, leave-me-alone teenager.

The woman knelt down to Elisha's eye level, and offered a business card. "I'm Margaret Jones. I work with the Light of Day Youth Shelter, just a few blocks from here." She looked toward Elijah. "Is he with you?"

35

Elisha shot her brother a sideways glance and shrugged. "I don't know. He's just sitting there and I'm sitting here."

She addressed both of them. "Well, if you need a place to stay tonight, we have rooms. We'll give you a good hot meal, a shower if you like, and your own room with your own bed, no questions asked."

Elijah asked, "What's the catch?"

"No catch. We're a charitable organization, we've been working the streets for nine years, and all we really want to do is get you off the street where you'll be safe and have some shelter."

Elijah, staying in character, gave a cynical sneer. "You're not the Living Way Youth Shelter? We've already been there."

The woman laughed apologetically and added, "No, no, we're somebody else, just a bunch of do-gooders, trying to help kids in trouble. You may like us, you may not, but at least you'll have a room for the night." She held out another business card.

Elijah accepted it with a shrug, then read it out loud. "Margaret Jones, Light of Day Youth Shelter, 203 Miller Street. Shelter, rescue, counseling."

Sarah entered the name and address on a laptop computer.

It could be perfectly legitimate, or it could be a very sly trap.

"I'm not getting any matches. I thought Living Way was the only youth shelter around here."

Nate carefully eyed the woman talking to his kids, thinking it over: no matches in the computer; no record of this particular youth shelter; a pleasant, nonthreatening woman with business cards.

It could be perfectly legitimate, or it could be a very sly trap. He spoke into his collar, "This could be it. Let's take it slow, one step at a time, and check it out."

3

truth and soup

I'm ready and willing," Elisha replied.

"It beats another night on the street," Elijah conceded, taking his sister's cue.

Margaret Jones thought they were talking to her. "Great! Come on, I'll walk you there." She started up the street at a leisurely pace and the kids followed her. "It can get rough out here. Not too many people who believe in Right and Wrong. You know what I mean?"

"Yeah," Elisha answered.

"Sure," said Elijah.

"But it looks like you two trust each other, and that's the start of friendship right there, doing right by our friends. You know what I'm talking about? Do you think there's a right and there's a wrong?"

They came to an intersection and turned right, heading up the hill.

"They've turned right on Spencer," Nate reported, walking a block behind them.

Sarah was behind the wheel and driving the van, watching a moving map on the dashboard linked with a GPS receiver. "Miller's three blocks north of Spencer on Second. I'll check it out." She turned up Spencer and drove right by her kids as they walked with Margaret Jones.

———————

Margaret Jones kept on talking, but there was something strangely "rehearsed" about it as if she was driving at something. "Some kids grow up going to church, things like that, and they seem to have a pretty good sense of right and wrong. Were either of you raised in church?"

Go with the flow, Elisha thought. "I was."

"Did you like it?"

"Sure."

"Do you believe in God?"

"Sure. I'm a Christian."

Margaret Jones was delighted. "You are? Well, that says a lot, doesn't it? I'll bet you're a very honest person then."

"I try to be."

"That's great. How about you . . . uh, what should I call you? You don't have to use your real name."

"Call me Jerry."

"Jerry, how about you? Do you believe in God?"

"Absolutely."

"So, do you think that helps you to be honest?"

He decided to act "dull" about it. "Sure, I guess."

"I mean, I've been wondering if a person's religious beliefs have anything to do with their morals. What do you think?"

———

Sarah drove past an old stone building cubbyholed between two newer ones and saw the little sign on the front window: Light of Day Youth Shelter. "I've found it and it looks real. I'm going to park somewhere."

"I still have the kids," Nate reported, following them up Second Avenue toward Miller.

Sarah parked against the curb a block past the shelter, shut down the engine, and clambered into the back where she once again manned the radio receivers and recording equipment.

———

"Here we are," said Margaret, pulling the door open.

Inside was a small reception area with chairs, couches, and a table neatly arranged with fashion, sports, and teen interest magazines. Through a wide archway to the right was a dining hall; several kids were sitting around the tables enjoying late-night soup and fresh baked bread. Through another wide archway to the left was a game and activity room; three boys and a girl were playing a game of pool, and Jay Leno was doing his opening monologue on television.

"Wow," said Elijah as they followed Margaret from room to room. "A game room, a pool table, a library . . ."

Elisha narrated as well. "Hey, you even have an elevator!"

"That takes you up to the rooms. Do you want to see your rooms first, or do you want to eat first?"

"Let's eat," said Elijah, and he wasn't acting.

———

Sarah opened the passenger door of the van to let a dirty vagrant enter.

He climbed into the expansive freight compartment, removed his coat and hat, then took a chair next to the radio console. From where they were parked, they had a good view of the shelter through the van's passenger window. They could hear the kids still talking, describing the place. "Looks like they're going to be warm and safe."

Sarah wagged her head. "Life is full of surprises."

Elisha's voice came over the radio as she conversed with Margaret. "So, how many kids are here?"

"At last count, I think around twenty. Some have been here for a week or so, and some are fresh off the street, like you. Grab a spoon. Bowls are over there."

"A game room, a pool table, a library . . ."

"I think I'll take these headphones off."

Sarah and Nate exchanged a glance. Elisha was letting them know she wouldn't be able to hear them for a while.

———

They sat at one of the dining tables with bowls of hot soup and slices of fresh bread, and Margaret sat down across from them.

Elisha muttered, "Who wants to say grace?"

Margaret smiled. "You go ahead."

Elisha bowed her head and prayed, "Dear Lord, thank you for this food and for a place to spend the night. In Jesus' name, Amen."

The kids got right down to the business of eating, trying to observe their surroundings and ask—or answer—questions between bites and slurps.

"It's nice to see kids who still say grace before they eat," Margaret commented.

"It's a God thing," said Elisha.

"So how long have you been on the road?" Margaret asked.

Elisha admitted, "A while."

"Yeah," Elijah muttered. "A while."

"So how's it been going?"

Elijah admitted, "Not great. We're both low on money, guess that's obvious, and stealing's wrong, so—"

"Really?"

He looked up from his soup. "Really what?"

"You believe stealing is wrong?"

44

He gave her a look. "Yeah. Is that news?"

She laughed. "Oh, no, not at all. But it's refreshing to see, especially under these circumstances. Say, I want to show you something." She slid two brochures across the table, one for each of them. "I don't show this to everybody, but you two are kind of special. Now, as always, there's no obligation . . ."

Well, thought Elijah, *now here's a new twist: a youth shelter with a sales presentation. We should have known there was a catch.*

What's it going to be? Elisha thought. *A vacation package? A time-share? Maybe they're recruiting people to sell candy door-to-door.*

Their thoughts came to a dead halt the moment their eyes fell upon the brochure's large, bold title.

Elijah picked up the brochure and opened it. It was a simple brochure, printed on glossy paper and folded into thirds, with color photographs. He read some of the copy inside: *A very special opportunity to be all you can be, and we pay the bill. Classes, activities, new friends . . .*

He was reading for information, of course, but also stalling for time, trying to make sure his voice would not quiver when he finally read the title out loud: "The Knight-Moore Academy."

As one, Nate and Sarah leaned forward, eyes wide open, pressing the headsets against their ears.

"Uhh . . . what is it?" Elisha asked, careful to control her voice.

"It's like a cross between a summer school and a summer camp," Margaret replied. "It's a place where kids just like yourselves can get away from the city, get away from distractions and hassles and just have the chance to, you know, get a grip on things. It's located in the woods, close to nature. We offer classes for high school credits, if you're interested—and if you want, counseling, guidance, discussion groups. And there are plenty of activities to blow off steam: sports, tennis, volleyball, a video arcade with all the latest games."

"And where is it?" Elijah asked.

"Up in the mountains, not far from here."

Elijah and Elisha looked at each other. Pay dirt.

Nate and Sarah looked at each other. Bingo.

Margaret came on like a saleslady. "It's free. Free room and board for as long as you need to stay—and you can maintain all the privacy you want. No one will ask you for your real name, or where you're from, or any other private information. The academy is there for you, just to give you time to sort things out, to find yourself."

"So who's paying for all this?" Elijah asked.

"It's a government pilot program, in its fifth year, the only one of its kind. It's kind of an experiment, actually. So, if you choose to participate, your feedback is going to be very important to us."

"And how do we get high school credit if we don't divulge our names or where we're from, or any other private information?" Elisha asked.

Margaret had to think a moment. "Um . . . well, if you want the credit, of course, you have the option to provide the information. But that's strictly up to you!"

Elijah read from the brochure for the benefit of those listening, "'A peaceful, thirty-acre campus deep in the heart of the national forest where guests can relax, restore, and then return to successful lives.' So can we leave whenever we want?"

"Of course."

Elijah yawned despite himself. After a hot meal so late at night, he was having trouble keeping his eyes open. "So how do we get there?"

"A bus leaves here every Sunday morning. If you decide you want to go, your timing couldn't be more perfect. You can spend the night and get on the bus in the morning."

Elisha was feeling way past ready for bed. "How early?"

Margaret smiled. "I think we can get the bus to hang around until you're awake. You both look pretty sleepy."

"You got that right."

"So, do you think you'd be interested?"

That was an easy question.

"Count me in," said Elisha.

"Sure," said Elijah. "I'll give it a try."

Sarah was already tapping the information into her computer. "I can't find any information on this place, either. Elisha, if you have your headphones on, let me know."

Elisha didn't respond. The three-way conversation just continued. They were leaving the table, heading for the elevator, talking about bed, sleep, soap, and towels.

Nate and Sarah heard the elevator door open, then close. It began lifting, the cables creaking. Then they heard Margaret's voice: "Jerry, you can take room 305. It's to the left and down near the end of the hall. Uh . . ."

"How about Sally?" Elisha said.

"Sally, I can show you your room."

Nate said, "They're going to get separated."

Sarah called, "Elisha, do you have your headphones on?"

Elisha's voice came back, pretending to talk to Margaret, "Pardon me for putting these on. I'm halfway through the final cut."

"No problem," said Margaret.

Nate and Sarah heard the elevator door open.

Sarah said, "We're going to check out the academy. Go ahead and get some sleep, and be sure to call us the moment you wake up in the morning."

Margaret was holding the elevator door open. Elisha stood in the elevator, eyes closed, apparently jiving with the music.

"This is your floor," Margaret prompted.

Elisha awoke from her groove. "Oh!" She looked sleepily at her brother and said, "Nighty-night, Jerry. Give us a call in the morning, won't you?"

He drew a sleepy sigh and acknowledged the message. "Will do."

Elisha stepped into the hall with Margaret, waved a lazy good-bye, and then the elevator door closed. Elijah rode the elevator up one more floor, then got out, turned left, and found 305. There was a bed ready and waiting, and soap and towels next to the sink. Nice room. Just like a college dorm.

He found a toothbrush in a plastic wrapper and managed to brush his teeth, but beyond that, he was just too sleepy. Without undressing, he flopped onto the bed, and that was the last thing he remembered.

Downstairs, in the kitchen, the cook carefully took Elijah's and Elisha's bowls, spoons, and glasses into a small office and closed the door. He set them in a neat pattern on the tabletop, took out a soft brush, and lightly dusted them with fine, black powder. Carefully holding a drinking glass up to the light, he nodded to himself. Good fingerprints.

About two in the morning, Nate and Sarah, asleep on narrow cots in the back of the van, were awakened by a loud rapping on the driver's window. Nate threw off his blankets and went up to the front.

There was a police officer standing outside, shining his flashlight in the window.

This kind of trouble they didn't need.

Nate had to squint into that offensive light as he rolled the window down a few inches. "Hello, officer."

"I'm sorry, but you can't park here. If you want to go up three blocks, there's space to park next to the on-ramp. I've seen some truckers stopping there for the night and so far there's no ordinance against it."

"Well, sure thing, officer. Thanks."

Sarah hated it. "We won't be able to keep an eye on the youth shelter."

"We'll just have to make it a short night and get back here first thing in the morning."

They drove away and found the spot the officer had told them about. Sarah double-checked the receiving equipment one last time. She and Nate could hear Elisha turn over in her bed, and they heard Elijah snoring. Satisfied the kids were safe for the night, they turned in.

The hallway was quiet, and most of the lights were out in Observation and Evaluation. One room was filled with doctors and nurses almost speechlessly treating a patient. A night nurse sat alone behind her small reception desk, working on paperwork by the light of a desk lamp, waiting for the rest of the night staff to return from their dinner break. From somewhere she could hear someone yelling. She looked up. Was that—

The elevator dinged, the door opened, and three men came stumbling, sliding, and wrestling out. The one in the middle, held tightly by the other two and struggling to get loose, was the one doing the yelling, his eyes wild, his mouth drooling. "Assassins! Assassins!"

Dressed in hospital whites, the two men trying to hold him were obviously hospital orderlies—and obviously on the wrong floor. "Which way to Safe Confinement?"

The nurse hurried into the hall, trying to be heard above the crazy man's hollering. "Fourth floor! *Fourth floor!*"

While the nurse was out in the hall, a tall, shadowy figure emerged quickly from the stairway door, slipped past her unoccupied desk, and into Observation and Evaluation. Keeping one ear tuned to the commotion, he hurried silently down the narrow hallway to a padded room, locked against the occupant's escaping, but easily opened from the outside. Silently, he entered and went to the bedside of a sleeping boy. He reached into a leather case at his side, selecting his instruments. This would not take long.

"Nate!"

It took several nudges before Nate realized it was Sarah who was nudging him. He rolled over on his cot, eyes still blurry, and muttered, "What time is it?"

"I'm not getting a signal."

"What do you mean?"

She went to the radio bench and fussed with the tuners. "There's no signal! They've quit transmitting!"

Nate rolled off his cot and took the chair next to her. The frequency was dead, nothing but static. He rechecked the tuners, rousing a mental checklist of possible causes from his sleepy memory. "Could be a number of things: the distance from the transmitters, the building the kids are in, where we're parked, power lines nearby . . ."

"Let's get over there."

He checked his watch. It was ten minutes after six in the morning. "Absolutely."

Sarah got to the driver's seat first. With a rumble and roar, the van came to life, and she steered for the Light of Day Youth Shelter, 203 Miller Street. The city block looked different in the morning light, but she thought she recognized the buildings as she drove

Silently, he entered and went to the bedside of a sleeping boy.

down the hill: the two newer ones, most likely office space, and then the old, stone building wedged between them, the . . .

The Dartmoor Hotel.

She eased the big van farther down the hill and parked in a loading zone. They hopped out and ran back.

The letters painted on the window and on the front door read, Dartmoor Hotel, followed by a phone number.

"Oh, okay," Nate said. "The youth shelter's using an old hotel. It makes sense."

"So why isn't their sign up in the window?"

"Uh . . . don't stare too long."

She forced herself to look away and appear detached. "What now?"

"Let's get back in the van. We might still get a signal, but if we don't we can wait for that bus to come for the kids, and then we can just make a visual contact." Nate started back. Sarah remained, looking through the window in the front door. "What?"

"It *is* a hotel," she said, her voice choked with foreboding.

He joined her and looked through the window as well. He could see a small lobby and a registration desk with a clerk sitting behind it. He took a step toward the door, looked more intently, and then walked toward the door with Sarah right beside him. He pushed the door open, they went inside . . .

It was a hotel lobby. A registration desk. A clerk. An old man sitting in a chair reading the paper. Potted plants. An old ceiling fan slowly spinning. There was no archway to the right that led to a dining hall; there was only a wall with a faded painting and two potted plants. There was an archway on the left, but there was no game and activity room beyond it, no pool table, no library, no television—only an empty banquet hall with yellowing wallpaper, peeling woodwork, and dirty, pedestal ashtrays.

The place was dead quiet. The clerk behind the registration desk looked bored, reading the paper. He didn't even look up to see who came in.

They approached the desk. "Excuse me?" Nate said.

The clerk looked up. He was a little man with a round head and thin, black hair. "Yes, can I help you?"

"We're looking for the Light of Day Youth Shelter."

The clerk looked at them blankly, then apologetically. "I'm sorry?"

Nate repeated, "We're trying to find the Light of Day Youth Shelter."

"Oh! There's a youth shelter down on Second, uh, Living Way, something like that—"

"No," said Sarah, quite edgy. "We're looking for the *Light of Day* Youth Shelter, the one at 203 Miller Street."

He looked at her quizzically again. "I guess you have the wrong address. This is the Dartmoor Hotel. It's been at this address for fifty years."

Nate was stuck for a moment, but then he chuckled, his face a little pink. "Sorry. We're in the wrong place."

He started for the door. Sarah needed a little prodding, so he took her arm. She almost objected, but he told her, "We've got the wrong building."

When they reached the sidewalk outside, she looked back. "Nate, this was it. This was the building!"

He was embarrassed. "It can't be! Come on, we'd better circle the block. We've got to find our kids before that bus comes."

He drove from the driver's seat and she "drove" from the passenger seat as they rounded the block, then tried the next block, then the next, then went up the hill to the next avenue and doubled back, circling all those blocks. They found no Light of Day Youth Shelter, nor any building that even resembled it, and of course, the address they'd copied down the night before had not changed. Wish as they might for a mistake, a misread, a different address in the morning light, it stubbornly remained 203 Miller Street.

A little after 7:00 in the morning, Nate parked the van across the street and half a block from the Dartmoor Hotel. Sarah went in the back and searched through the recording they'd made the night before until she found Elijah's voice reading the address off Margaret Jones's business card: "203 Miller Street."

Then she and Nate sat silently in the front seat of the van, staring, wondering, as the recording kept playing and they heard the voices of Elijah and Elisha describing the game room, the kitchen, the dining hall. They could hear the voices of young people in the background, laughter, talking, dishes clinking, the distant *clack* of pool balls hitting each other, the goofy one-liners of Jay Leno opening the *Tonight Show*.

They were trying to think instead of panicking.

Then they heard Margaret's voice telling Elijah, "Jerry, you can take room 305."

They were out of the van in an instant, dashing across the street, up the block, and down the narrow alley. The Dartmoor Hotel had a back stairway. They went up the stairs as quickly as quiet would allow, then stole down the third-floor hallway. It was messy. Trash lay on the old carpet, and graffiti marred the walls.

They found the door to room 305. Inside, a radio was playing softly.

Sarah knocked on the door. "Uh . . . Jerry?"

A woman's voice answered from inside, "Who is it?"

Then a man's gruff voice rumbled, "Whatever you're selling, we don't want any!"

Back in the front seat of the van, Nate and Sarah were speechless for an unnatural length of time.

"It's like I'm having a nightmare," said Sarah, "and I can't wake up."

"Like we're going crazy," said Nate, staring at the building across the street.

Then Sarah almost whispered, "'I don't know.'"

"What don't you know?"

"No, no, the *boy in the hospital*. He kept saying 'I don't know' as if . . ."

Nate caught her meaning—". . . as if all knowledge and logic were gone."

"As if he's been *here*. We're in another world, Nate. I know we followed the kids here last night . . . but now that isn't true anymore. It's as if someone's trying to erase my memory, maybe even my sanity."

They both fell silent. They were thinking.

Nate finally commented, "Whoever they are, they're very good at what they do."

Sarah's voice tightened with fear. "And they have our kids."

Nate punched in a number on the van's cell phone, switching it to speakerphone so they could both converse.

Mr. Morgan answered on the second ring. "Nate, I was going to call you—"

"Morgan, I want you to tell us we're not going crazy."

There was silence, and then a sigh at the other end. "What's happened?"

"Reality is shifting before our very eyes!" Sarah told him.

Nate quickly recapped what had happened, then said, "So we've tracked the kids to a certain point, and . . ."

"And . . . ?"

"The kids aren't there—but that point isn't there anymore, either. It's gone, like it never existed." Nate raised his voice, his anger apparent. "Morgan, who in the world are we dealing with?"

There was another significant pause before Morgan replied, "I have one clue for you: Alvin Rogers, the boy in the hospital, is dead. The death certificate will undoubtedly say it was a massive heart attack. But I'm quite sure he was murdered."

"It's like I'm having a nightmare," said Sarah, "and I can't wake up."

4

waking up in nightmare

Elijah began to wake up, but very slowly. He'd already spent several rough days and nights hanging out on the streets of Seattle without much sleep, and now he was paying for it. His body felt like lead, and he could hardly open his eyes.

He became aware of his clothes, the same clothes he'd been wearing for days. Now he'd worn them all night, and if he didn't get a shower and something fresh to wear, he was going to be one very smelly "runaway." Then he became aware of something else: kids' voices laughing, cheering, hollering, as if a rollicking game was going on. Yes, he could hear the distinctive sound of a volleyball being batted about.

Volleyball in the middle of the city?

He opened his eyes. Sunshine was pouring in through the window, warm and dazzling. It made him squint.

He raised his head and looked around. He didn't remember this room very well, but, of course, he was so sleepy last night he

Volleyball in the middle of the city?

wasn't paying much attention. It wasn't large, just a typical hotel room. It looked cleaner than he remembered. The walls and ceiling were painted white, and an attractive blue carpet was on the floor. His bed was set against one wall, and against another wall were a small dresser and a desk.

He sat up on the bed, pausing a moment to let some dizziness pass. He didn't remember the dresser or the desk from last night. On the other hand, he did remember brushing his teeth in a small bathroom that now appeared to be a closet.

With some effort, he rose to his feet and went to the window.

He froze where he stood, hardly breathing, nothing moving but his eyes as he scanned left and right, taking in scenery he wasn't ready to believe.

He was looking out on what appeared to be a summer camp. Immediately outside the window was a wide-open field of green grass—a baseball diamond, a soccer and football field, and a volleyball court where a good-sized bunch of kids were having a rollicking game, volleying and spiking the ball over the net. The field was bordered on all four sides by campus structures that reminded him of a YMCA camp, most likely a dining hall, recreation building, maybe some classrooms, and dormitories like the one he was standing in right now. Beyond all of it were steep, forested hills, possibly mountains—from this window he couldn't see their tops.

There'd been a change during the night.

Elijah immediately checked himself over, patting his pockets. Everything was still there: a little spare change, a handkerchief, half a stick of gum, and especially the small radio transmitter he was wearing under his shirt. A mirror hung on the wall just opposite the closet. He studied his reflection, but apart from looking like a street bum who'd slept in his clothes all night, he found nothing of concern. As far as he could tell, his body and everything on it had not been disturbed, simply moved.

He searched his memory and found it disappointingly blank. He remembered he and Elisha did agree to give the Knight-Moore Academy a try, but he hadn't the slightest memory of how they got from that moment and that place to this one.

They? He was immediately concerned for Elisha.

Knock knock knock! A male voice called from outside the door, "Hello? Jerry? You awake?"

Okay, Elijah told himself, *I'm still Jerry.* "Uh, who is it?"

"Clyde Stern, the dorm superintendent. Let's go; you've got a meeting with the dean in five minutes."

Elijah opened the door. The man standing outside was well-built, in his thirties, with brown, curly hair and a smile that looked a little grim. He was dressed a bit formal, in burgundy blazer, white shirt, black slacks, and black tie. Elijah felt like a slob just being in his presence. The man made a face as if he were *looking* at a slob. "Where's your uniform?"

"I, I don't know about any uniform."

He was immediately concerned for Elisha.

Stern looked past Elijah into the room. "Don't give me that. It's right there in your closet."

Elijah ventured a look in the closet, and there it was: a burgundy blazer, black slacks, white shirt, and black tie, all freshly pressed and ready to go.

"What have you been doing all morning?" Stern demanded. "Bingham's gonna have a cow!"

"Who?"

"Mr. Bingham. The dean. Remember?"

"Guess I'd better change—"

Stern just yanked on Elijah's shirtsleeve. "No time, kid. Bingham doesn't wait."

Elijah followed Stern, walking briskly down the hall because it was the only thing he knew to do. The hall was messy; litter and clothing were lying about, and there was graffiti on the walls. Considering Stern's snappy, uniformed, hop-to-it manner, the condition of this place didn't make a lot of sense. Oh, well. Nothing was making much sense yet. Elijah's mind was still fuzzy, he could definitely smell himself, and he was still trying to catch up with . . . well, everything.

"What about that girl who was with me?" he asked.

"She's gonna meet us there."

"So she's okay?"

Stern looked at him with that same judgmental eye. "She's great. In a lot better shape than you right now."

They went out a door and into the sunshine, taking a walkway that led across the campus.

Stern waved toward the volleyball game. "Hey, Easley!"

Easley looked like a typical coach. He was young and athletic, dressed in black shorts and burgundy tee shirt. He waved from the sidelines of the game. "So that's the new guy?"

"Yeah. Isn't he a mess?"

Now the whole game stopped and about thirty kids took a moment to stare at the mess. He looked back, waving hello. The friendly ones waved; the rest didn't look friendly. They came in all colors, types, and sizes, with short hair, long hair, no hair, frizzed hair, purple hair, dreadlocked hair. Some were jocks and proud of it, some were flirts and proud of that, some were just followers, not proud of anything. They were all dressed in the same outfit as the coach: black shorts, burgundy tee shirts, snazzy running shoes.

"Come on," said a big guy holding the ball. It was his serve. "Let's get on with the game!"

They all went back to their game, and Elijah and Mr. Stern kept walking.

"I take it this is the Knight-Moore Academy?" Elijah asked.

"This is the place," said Stern. "That's the library right there— you can check out books, CDs, videos, whatever you want. That building over there is the recreation hall. They've got pool tables, Ping-Pong, foozball, video games, lots of stuff. That's the dining hall, three squares a day. We have four dorm buildings, A, B, C, and D. A and B are where you just came from, over there. A's for girls, B's for boys, so you're in B. Over on the other side there are two more: C's for girls, D's for boys. Don't get 'em mixed up."

The buildings looked new and freshly painted—basic white,

with burgundy trim; all the lawns were neatly kept; the planting beds along the buildings, though small, were weeded and flowers were blooming. The scenery all around the place was spectacular: mountains, tall forests, even some snow-covered peaks in the distance.

"Where is this place?"

Stern just waved off the question. "In the mountains, up in the trees. Don't worry about it."

"So how did I get here?"

Stern made a face at that question. "Man, you'd better get tuned in. You rode the bus up here. Don't tell me you don't remember."

"I *don't* remember."

He only chuckled and sneered. "I can believe it. We get a lot of your kind in here, so strung out they don't remember anything. But don't worry about it."

Elijah had been eyeing one thing that looked a little out of place: At the far edge of the athletic field was a high stone wall with a big iron gate, and on the forested hill beyond that wall, surrounded by green lawns and lush gardens, stood an impressive mansion with ornate gables, complex corners, and tall windows. "What in the world is that place?"

"You don't want to go there," said Stern.

"But what is it?"

"Where is this place?"

"It's the headquarters for—oh, brother, not again!" Stern stopped, exasperated, looking at some garbage cans knocked over and rolled about, their contents strewn all over the grass and sidewalk. "This is getting serious!"

Elijah ventured, "Looks like you have some bears around here."

"You got that right. They're getting to be a real problem. Hey, by the way, get a clue: Don't go into the woods, okay? Just stay on the campus, stay right here on the grounds. Had a gal last summer just about got her face torn off. It was terrible."

"Right," Elijah answered, chilled by the warning. "But if there are bears around, why are you using conventional garbage cans? I mean, any bear that wants to can pop these right open—"

"All right, here comes that girlfriend of yours."

Elijah looked up the sidewalk and the sight made his day: His sister—well, make that *girl acquaintance going by the name Sally* coming their way, accompanied by a small, bookish woman in a female version of the standard Knight-Moore uniform: burgundy blazer, black skirt, white blouse, black scarf. *Somebody made a fortune selling uniforms to this place.*

Elisha was wearing the same thing, and looked great, a far cry from the street kid she'd been portraying the night before. Her face was clean, her washed hair, still jet-black, was blowing in the breeze. She looked like a posh, private-school girl. She broke into a big smile when she saw him. "Hey, you're alive!"

"Pretty much," he answered, deciding not to run and hug her.

"You look like dirt."

"Yeah, rub it in."

"Jerry, this is Mrs. Meeks."

He extended his hand and she greeted him. "Welcome to Knight-Moore, Jerry. Did you have a pleasant trip?"

"Well, actually, I—"

"Step this way," said Mr. Stern. "Mr. Bingham's waiting."

Stern and Meeks led them—they felt herded, actually—through a nearby doorway marked "OFFICE." They passed by a front office with a counter, some desks, lots of papers lying around, and a computer but no one there at the moment. Then they hurried down the central hallway, Elijah and Elisha in front, their hosts right behind them, maintaining a brisk pace.

"You feeling okay?" Elisha asked in a near whisper.

"Kind of woozy," Elijah answered.

"Me, too."

A door at the end of the hall stood open, and through that door they saw a man sitting behind a desk, hands folded, looking over his reading glasses at them. His hair was a fright wig of black and gray, he was definitely on the paunchy side, and he seemed to be studying them before they even got there. Stern and Meeks whisked them through the door, guided them to two chairs in front of Bingham's desk, and went out, closing the door behind them. *Slam!*

They sat still, exchanging a look, feeling like two newspapers tossed on someone's doorstep.

"Hello," Mr. Bingham said in a slow, sweeping manner. "Welcome to Knight-Moore Academy. You do not have to give me your real names. I am Mr. Bingham, the academy dean."

"Hi," they said.

He eyed them with a strange fascination, his gaze shifting from one to the other and back. "Young lady, if you weren't so beautiful, and young man, if you weren't so disgusting, the two of you could be twins."

They looked at each other, did some mental comparisons, and then laughed. Great joke.

Mr. Bingham wasn't laughing. "Young man, you do have a uniform, don't you?"

"I wasn't aware of it until five minutes ago."

"Uniforms are one of the few requirements we have here. They're important, don't you see, to maintain comradeship among the students, to eliminate any semblance of superiority. We are all equals here."

Elisha asked, "Mr. Bingham, just where is this place?"

He smiled, leaned over his desk, and asked over his reading glasses, "Where would you like it to be?" They looked at each other, searching for an answer, but he just kept going. "I don't mean to evade your question, but starting now, you must consider this a rare opportunity to create your own world the way you would have it. Wherever you came from—and I don't care to

He eyed them with a strange fascination, his gaze shifting from one to the other and back.

know where, thank you—you were confined to and controlled by the expectations of those around you: parents, teachers, church, and so forth. You did what they told you, you believed what they told you, and Truth, well, Truth was theirs, not yours. Are you with me thus far?"

Elijah started to say, "Well, no, not really . . ."

But Bingham just kept going. "But, of course, you fled from that, didn't you? Here you are, run away from home, trying to find your own way, a world, a truth that fits you better than what you had at home. Well, . . ." He stood behind his desk and held his lapels. "Consider this the first real step of your journey. Here is where you can think for yourself, find out for yourself, study for yourself, and find your own truth, whatever you want it to be."

"My own truth?" Elisha asked, eyebrows up.

"You're certainly permitted to be yourself if you so choose, but if you so choose, you can be somebody else. What matters is that you are happy with whom and what you've decided to be."

He began to walk slowly around the room, studying them from different angles. "As part of this process, you can, if you wish, attend optional classes for high school credit. We offer classes in English, remedial reading, humanities, math, history, art . . ." He passed them each a list of classes and a schedule. "Pick out what you like, but don't delay. You're coming in a few days late, I'm sure you realize that.

"Also, as part of the process, we require participation in discussion circles with Mr. Easley, a chance for you to toss around new ideas and for us to gauge how well we're doing. There will be a discussion circle in Mr. Easley's classroom at 1:30. Please be there.

"Everyone is a guest here, but for your own safety, this is a closed campus, and there can be no leaving. We're out in the middle of hostile wilderness, with national forest for miles in all directions. If you venture too far into those woods, you could become lost and we would have no way to find you. And besides . . . I suppose you've already seen indications of our bear problem? We not only have bears, we have cougars, and the only safe place is within the boundaries of the campus. Are you with me thus far?"

"Are there telephones?" Elijah asked.

"Oh, heavens, no. That would bring in the outside world, and that would taint everything we're trying to accomplish here."

"But what are you trying to accomplish?"

"No doubt you have noticed the mansion on the hill."

"Sure have," said Elijah. "What's up there?"

"The mansion is off-limits; be absolutely certain of that. This campus is your home, the mansion belongs to your faculty and leadership. We all have our own little kingdoms, don't you see: You have yours here, we have ours there. Respect that. Agreed?"

They nodded. "Agreed."

"Now. It's safe to assume that you have very little money." Bingham brought out two small, cloth bags closed with draw-strings. "These are Knight-Moore dollars." He handed each of them a bag. Inside were shiny metal coins the size of a quarter, light in weight, probably made of tin or aluminum. On one side was the "value," 1 KM Dollar, and on the other side were fancy letters, KM, with "The Knight-Moore Academy" inscribed around the outside. Elijah was expecting to see Mr. Bingham's profile, but no.

"These are the academy currency," Bingham continued, "good for purchases at the Campus Exchange, treats from the cafeteria vending machines, games in the Rec Center, and so forth. It's an additional measure to provide our own in-house economy while discouraging theft and greed. Each of you gets twenty-five KMs to start. You can earn more, spend it all; it's up to you."

He sank into his chair again and looked across his desk at them. "On behalf of the faculty and staff, I bid you welcome."

"Thank you," they answered, still bewildered.

The door opened again, on cue, and Mr. Stern and Mrs. Meeks ushered them out of the office and back down the hall toward the front door.

"I'm over in dorm B," said Elijah. "Where are you staying?"

"Dorm C, room 4, facing the playfield. What's your room number?"

"Room 6," Stern answered for Elijah, then told him, "Come on, I'll walk you back, show you the showers."

"Where will you be?" Elijah asked Elisha.

"Watching the volleyball game," said Mrs. Meeks. "Come, Sally, I'll introduce you to the others."

Morgan's face spoke from the screen on Sarah's laptop. "All right. Hello. Is the signal clear?"

Nate and Sarah, in the back of their big van, answered, "Yes. We can see you clearly."

"Good. I can see you as well. We'll have to communicate through this discrete system for the time being and not trust the telephones. Someone knew all they needed to know to kill Alvin Rogers: his whereabouts, his condition, the layout of the hospital, who the nurse was on the night shift, everything. Let's not help our adversaries any further."

"Who are they?" Nate asked.

"We still don't know, and we still need you to find out. Apparently, Alvin Rogers could have told us once he regained his sanity."

"Morgan," said Sarah, "they have our children."

"They mustn't know it. They have to think they've picked up two runaways, not two investigators. Keep in mind that whoever it is could have spies in the sheriff's department, the police, the Bureau for Missing Children, the hospital staff—anyone and everyone who had anything to do with Alvin Rogers."

"So we can't talk to the hospital," Sarah lamented.

"Or the police, or the sheriff. And until we can find out more about this Nelson Farmer character, I wouldn't go anywhere near the BMC. To do so would give someone a clue that your kids are not what they appear to be."

"You're not making this easy," said Nate.

"I'll do all I can to make it less difficult."

"We'll be in touch."

"Good-bye."

The image blinked off the screen, leaving Nate and Sarah feeling very alone.

Sarah wasn't about to sit still, not with her kids missing. "Nate, we have to trust *somebody*."

"How about our friends at the youth shelter—the *real* one?"

———————

Elisha definitely had that "new girl in school" feeling as she approached the volleyball game. Mrs. Meeks kept a motherly hand on her shoulder to encourage—or perhaps force—her along, until she stood next to Mr. Easley, who said a quick hello. None of the kids playing the game paid her any mind. The game was getting intense, coming down to the wire. The ball was sailing over the net and bouncing off hands at a frantic pace, and the yells and screams were reaching one big, unintelligible roar.

Bap! A girl swatted the ball over the net.

Bip, bap, the ball bounced from one player's hands to the next, and then *bump!* it hit the ground. A tall white guy with a nearly shaved head scooped it up and put it back into play.

"Hey!" came some protests from the opposing team, but the game kept going.

Bip, bap, bung, bat, the ball bounced from one player to the next, and then *Bam!* a big, muscular guy spiked it back.

It shot like a cannonball between two players and bounded off the ground. Everybody on that side wailed in defeat—and disgust.

Mr. Easley sounded his whistle. "Okay, that's it. That's game, twenty-one to eighteen. Good job!"

"No fair!" a black girl in dreadlocks wailed, pointing at the tall white guy. "The ball hit the ground before he hit it!"

The culprit on the other side retorted, "You played on it."

"So?" said the black girl's companion, a stocky Hispanic who must have cut her own hair.

"Ah, but listen," said Mr. Easley. He had to blow his whistle to get their attention. "Listen. See what you're doing? You're falling into that old trap again, trying to see things as either/or."

Elisha wasn't sure what he was talking about, but some of the kids rolled their eyes when he said it.

"Aren't you?" Easley prodded. "You're saying, 'Either they won or we did.'"

"They didn't!" said the black girl.

"We *did*," said the tall white guy.

"See?" said Easley. "That's either/or. But let me ask you this: Did you enjoy the game?"

"Yeah, 'til a few seconds ago," said the little Hispanic.

"Then it was an experience, wasn't it?" He raised his voice so everyone could hear. "You have power over the experience, to make it what you want, so it's the experience that matters. If you enjoyed playing the game, then you've already won as long as you think you've won. You can all be winners and the score doesn't have to mean anything. That's both/and." He asked the little Hispanic, "Come on, Maria, see if you can say it using both/and."

Maria gave a grumpy sigh and attempted it. "*Both* our team *and* their team won."

There was a collective moan from several. "Oh right, yeah!" "No way." "Sore losers, that's all."

"But *we* won!" said a chubby gal on the "losing" side.

"You're right!" said Easley.

Another moan, and some pretty hot protests.

"And *you're* right!" he told the moaners, which cheered only half of them. "Listen. If the experience was yours and you enjoyed it, then you won. There's no winning or losing here, no right or wrong. There's just the game and what you make of it."

A cute blond with wire-rimmed glasses hopped in the air and squeaked, "I won!"

A few of her teammates—all from the "losing" side—tried to match her enthusiasm. "We won." "Yeah, right, we won."

"We all won," the tall guy finally conceded.

"Until next time," said the muscular guy, and several of his teammates agreed with him.

Easley called out, "Hey, this is the new girl. Let's make her welcome." He asked Elisha, "What name would you like?"

Elisha was confused by the question. "What name? Oh. I guess, Sally."

"Everybody, this is Sally."

Girls and boys came forward, shaking her hand. "Hi, Sally." "Hi, Sally." "Hi, Sally."

"Hi. Hi. Hi."

The cute blond with the wire-rimmed glasses stepped up with springs in her feet. "Hi. Are you the new girl in room 4?"

"Yes."

"Cool! We're roommates, did you know that?"

Elisha smiled. "So *you're* Alice! Mrs. Meeks was telling me about you."

The girl laughed. "I was Alice yesterday. I'm Marcy today."

"Oh . . . okay. Marcy."

"I'm from Maine. I've always wanted to be from there. I hear it's pretty. Who are you today? Are you somebody?"

"I . . . I guess I'm just myself."

"Whoa! I'm not ready for that one yet."

Then two sizable jocks stepped up, the big, muscular guy and a good-looking, surfer type.

"Hey," said Muscles, looking her over and enjoying it, "the name's Alex. I'm glad you could be here to see us win."

"We *all* won," said the surfer.

Alex glared at him. "Brett, who said you could stand here?"

Brett came right back, with fight in his eyes, "I stand where I want."

Alex only smiled as if amused. "We'll see."

Brett pointed his finger in Alex's face. "Next time."

"Next time," Alex agreed.

Brett extended his hand. "It's nice to meet you, Sally." With a quick nod toward Alex he added, "Be careful." Then, with a parting dagger-eye at Alex, he left.

Alex confided, "He's got a few problems—being a loser's one of them. Hey, if there's anything you need, you know who to call."

Mr. Easley came near, wearing that perpetually kind smile. "You're going to have a great time here. Don't worry about anything. We're all friends."

Really? thought Elisha. *Two roosters about to spur each other, and—*

"Come on, Sally," said Marcy-for-today, "let's go get our room set up just the way we want it, like our own little world."

—and one sweet person who's afraid to be herself, Elisha finished her thought.

"Are you Sally for today, or are you always Sally?"

"I'm . . ." *So how do I answer this one?* "Well, I'm Sally for now. How about that?"

"Cool."

Weird, Elisha thought. *Here I am, playing a role, but so is everybody else! Dear Lord, I'm going to need your help with this one.*

5

"what's yours is mine"

A little before noon, the Dartmoor Hotel had an unexpected visitor, a balding, middle-aged man carrying a briefcase and wearing a suit and tie. He came through the front door, paused to look around the lobby, and then walked slowly to the reception desk where the little man with the thin, black hair and round head was still sitting, reading his newspaper. "Good morning," said the visitor.

"All the rooms are full," said the man behind the desk.

The visitor was disappointed. "You sure? I've come a long way, and this place is nice and close to where I have to do my business."

"Sorry. You might try up the street. The Sullivan or the Royal Arms."

The visitor looked around one more time. "So, what do you do here? You rent rooms by the week, the month? You got apartments up there?" Without warning, he pressed the button for the elevator.

"Hey! You can't go up there!"

The door to the old elevator slid open. "I might be interested in an apartment. Why don't you show me one?"

"We're in the middle of a renovation. There's nothing to see up there."

The visitor stood still and let the elevator door slide shut again. "Aw, that's too bad. Well, like you say, I'll try the Sullivan. Thanks, anyway."

He walked toward the door, but turned right to have a look at the empty room through the archway. Satisfied, he gave a detached shrug and went out the door.

He walked casually up the street, whistling to himself, his briefcase swinging at his side, and then turned into an alley where a large van was waiting. He hopped in and the van rolled down the alley.

Sarah was behind the wheel and gave him a thumbs-up. "Perfect. I think we got it all."

The man squeezed between the two front seats and hurried into the back of the van, pulling a hidden radio transmitter from under his shirt. "I haven't seen that guy around here before, and I hope he hasn't seen me."

Nate was in back, manning all the electronic surveillance gear. "Charlie, if we're right about that so-called hotel, I doubt either of you have seen each other before. Our little hotel clerk is nothing but an actor." He began tapping away at the computer and clicking the mouse, isolating certain sounds from a recording they'd

"Hey! You can't go up there!"

just made. "Now I'll just stack all these sounds in a file." *Click.* *Click.* "And pull up our other file . . ." *Click. Click-click.* "And compare the two."

The van eased to a stop. Sarah turned off the engine, set the brake, and came back to join them.

"I think we're going to find exactly what we were expecting," said Nate as he played the first recording.

They heard the sound of a latch opening, the squeak of hinges, the quiet rush of a door moving across a carpet.

"That's you, Charlie, going in the front door," Nate said.

Next they heard the very same sounds repeated.

Sarah sat up straight in her chair. "Is it . . . ?"

Nate nodded. "That was the kids going through the same door last night. Let's check the next one."

A series of wooden squeaks, then another. The second recording involved more feet, but the squeaks were virtually the same.

"Same floor," Nate said, "last night and today."

A rumble, the ding of a bell, a door sliding open. The same sounds again.

"Same elevator," said Sarah.

"This next one's a little tougher," said Nate, raising the volume.

What they mainly heard was "air noise," the sound of a particular room. Then they heard another sample.

Nate put both sounds on the computer screen so they appeared as wavy lines. "Yes, same wave structure. And look here." He pointed at a little spike that appeared in both sound waves. "The floor makes that same squeak right as you go under the archway. So guess what, Sarah?" He spun in his chair to look at her. "We're not crazy."

She shook her head in wonder. "Incredible."

Charlie nodded toward the outside. "So how about a bite to eat? It's about that time. We'll talk."

They climbed out of the van, stepping into a narrow alley and up to a plain little door with a neatly worded sign: Living Way Youth Shelter. Everyone Welcome.

Charlie led the way through the door, through a storeroom and pantry, through a kitchen, and into a dining hall where nearly a dozen kids were starting their lunch.

Anita, Charlie's wife, was just getting the kids' attention. "Okay, put the spoons down. We're going to pray." The kids put down their spoons and bowed their heads. Nate, Sarah, and Charlie bowed their heads as well. "Dear Lord, we thank you for this food and for this home. Please warm our hearts as we feed our bodies. Amen."

The kids started slurping their soup and passing the bread around as Nate, Sarah, and Charlie found a table over in the corner where they could talk.

Charlie Ramirez and his wife, Anita, started the Living Way shelter six years ago as a ministry to runaways and wayward kids with nowhere else to go. Abused kids, rebellious kids, kids on drugs, kids just plain scared—Charlie and Anita handled them all.

"I've never heard any of the kids talk about another youth shelter in town," Charlie said in a quiet, cautious voice. "I never had any idea. . . ."

"Could you start asking around?" asked Sarah. "The way

these kids circulate on the street, somebody had to have heard something."

"And ask them if they ever encountered a woman named Margaret Jones," said Nate.

"Discreetly," Sarah added. "You can see what we're up against."

Charlie nodded intently. "I'll ask the ones here, and we can check with the ones who've gone home. We have a follow-up list, so we can call them."

"And ask if anyone's ever heard of the Knight-Moore Academy, or anything that sounds like that. We heard Elijah and Elisha talking about it, but we're not sure of the correct spelling."

"This Margaret Jones woman showed the kids a brochure," said Nate. "We need to get our hands on it."

By now, Charlie was making a list. "Oh, dear Jesus, help us."

———

When Elijah showed up for the discussion circle with Mr. Easley at 1:30, he looked sharp. The academy had provided a toiletry kit, so he'd made good use of it. He'd showered, combed his hair, shaved whatever whiskers he could find, and gotten into his uniform, which, interestingly, fit him perfectly. It made him wonder, *How did these people know my exact measurements? Did they come*

"Oh, dear Jesus, help us."

into the room with a tape measure while I was asleep? Eeuugh! What a creepy thought.

Well, anyway, now he was dressed properly, ready to fit in with the others—or so he thought.

First surprise: The discussion circle wasn't meeting in the scheduled classroom. A sign taped to the door told everyone the group would be meeting out on the grass near the edge of the campus, in the shade of some tall cedars. He looked across the open field and saw them already gathered, with some stragglers still ambling across the grass. He ran.

Second surprise: Now that he looked sharp, everybody else looked sloppy. Yes, they were wearing their uniforms—sort of— but many had their shoes off, almost all of them had shed their blazers, and only a few were still wearing ties. Shoes, ties, and blazers were lying about on the grass, and the kids were lounging around in a very rough circle facing Mr. Easley, who was still in his tee shirt and black shorts.

Mr. Easley smiled at him. "Hey, uh . . . what's your name today?"

"Jerry. Sorry I'm late."

"Hey, there's no such thing as being late to discussion circle. Everybody comes when they feel like it. You do what you feel. Have a seat somewhere, wherever you want. Oh, and Jerry!" Elijah stopped, and Mr. Easley tossed him a KM dollar. "That's for showing up."

He quickly scanned the group and found Elisha with a blond friend under an ancient cottonwood. He settled on the grass near her, but not right next to her, catching a welcome from her eyes.

"Take your tie off, if you want," said Easley. "I know the academy has a rule about wearing uniforms, but as I've told the others, what are we really trying to do here? We want everyone to be equal, sure, but we're also trying to cut everybody loose, let everybody have their own life. If you have to wear a uniform all the time, then you're just being squished into the same mold as everybody else, and we don't want that either, right?"

"Right!" the group agreed.

"Now. What were we talking about?"

"Whatever we wanted," said a tough-looking street dude who'd rolled up his sleeves to show off his tattoos.

"That's the stuff, Ramon!" Easley tossed Ramon another KM. "We were talking about possessions."

"And stealing," said a purple-haired scarecrow of a girl. "Like, if people don't want to share their stuff, maybe it's okay to *make* 'em share it."

"By taking things?" asked a somewhat miffed, stringy-haired blond.

"Hey, if I want something, why shouldn't I have it?"

"Because maybe it belongs to me, that's why!" She told Mr. Easley, "Somebody stole my Walkman and I don't appreciate it one bit."

"Was it really yours?" Easley asked.

"Of course it was mine!"

"So you paid for it, or someone gave it to you?"

Now the girl shrank a bit. "No. I found it."

"Oh-hooo!" the group reacted. Gotcha.

Easley held up a hand. "Well now, come on, let's not get into *either/or* here, as if *either* Charlene *or* Melinda is right. Maybe *both* Charlene *and* Melinda are right. Maybe the real problem is private possessions. Charlene believes that all the world is community property and everybody owns it, right?"

Charlene gave her gum a few thoughtful chomps, and then flipped some purple hair out of her eyes. "Yeah. Sounds good."

"But it looks like Melinda agrees with you—at least she did when she, uh, *found* the Walkman, didn't you, Melinda?"

Melinda got a little flustered and looked at the ground as she replied, "I don't know. I just wanted it, that's all."

"Nothing wrong with that," said Ramon.

She turned on him. "Yeah, so how would you like it if somebody ripped off *your* stuff?"

"Oooohh," the group reacted, mocking her anger.

Easley tossed both girls a coin and then held up a hand to calm things down. "Okay, now Melinda's asked Ramon the big question: How would I like it? Well, that's up to each of us, isn't it? If I'm being selfish with things, then sure, I'm going to get upset if someone else needs what I want to keep for myself. Melinda, did it ever occur to you that perhaps you're being too selfish with things? Do you think it's fair for you to have a Walkman when somebody else doesn't?"

"Yeah, Melinda," piped up some others, "what about that?"

"You could look at it this way: You're actually sharing; you just don't know it. I think that's the whole point here: If nobody owns anything, then how can anyone steal it?"

Melinda looked around the group, still angry and suspicious. "Well if that's the way you want to say it, then whoever's sharing my Walkman, I'd like it if you'd share it back again."

"All right," said Mr. Easley. "See? Both Melinda and Charlene are right."

"Do I get another dollar?"

Easley tossed Melinda another "dollar," then applauded as the kids laughed and cheered.

Elijah chuckled and muttered to himself, "Either/or."

Easley heard him. "What was that, Jerry?"

Elijah was on the spot. He could feel every eye on him. "Oh, nothing. That was just an either/or, that's all."

"What was?"

Elijah wasn't the kind to shrink from a direct question. "Well, you're trying to tell us that *both* Melinda *and* Charlene are right, but that was never the case. All you did was argue with Melinda to get her to change her mind, so that means, *either* she saw stealing as sharing *or* she was selfish. It wasn't a both/and; it was an either/or."

Now a few "oh-hos" arose toward Mr. Easley, and Elijah even heard a fellow say, "He's got you there."

By now, Elisha's mental stew was about to boil over, so she jumped in. "And I'm not even sure she's changed her mind."

Melinda just looked at the coin in her hand and said, "Yeah. I guess so," although her eyes were still the resentful eyes of someone who'd been ripped off.

Elisha was on a roll. "I don't think she should change her mind. Sure, it's good to share, and we shouldn't be selfish, but calling stealing sharing doesn't make it sharing, it's still stealing, and stealing is wrong, and if Melinda stole that Walkman, she was ripping somebody off, and whoever took her Walkman without her permission was ripping *her* off."

There were some hoots and disagreements—"Hey, welcome to the real world," "Preach it!" But there were some firm agreements as well—"Hey, a ripoff's a ripoff," "I wouldn't want somebody stealing my stuff"—and even some applause.

Easley just smiled. "Sally, you're new here, so it'll take some time for you to catch up. I think all of us have been raised with certain ideas of right and wrong, but now we can build our own world right here, and create a new truth."

Elisha looked at him strangely. "A new truth? Like what?"

He smiled, pleased at the thought. "Whatever we agree on. You see, Right and Wrong are what we choose to make them."

Elijah piped up—he couldn't help it. "Is that statement you just made right or wrong?"

Easley didn't appear to appreciate the question. "It depends on what the group thinks." Easley looked around at the group. "How about it? Do we agree?"

"Sure," they replied. "Yeah." "Whatever." "Sounds good."

He tossed them some more coins.

"So now it's what the group thinks?" Elijah asked. "What if the group decided you're wrong? Would you still be right?"

"Well, I can still have any truth I want in my own mind," Easley admitted.

"So you can have it both ways at the same time."

"Exactly! Both/and!"

Elijah looked at Elisha. "Then stealing really *is* wrong!" Then he looked at Melinda. "And you really *were* ripped off!"

The group began laughing, mostly at Easley's frustrated look.

"No, no, not really!" Easley argued. "Not if the group doesn't think so!"

"No? Not really?" Elijah furrowed his brow, working up his answer. "So *either* stealing is wrong and Melinda got ripped off, *or* the group is right and she's just sharing."

Easley countered, "*Both* Melinda *and* the group are right."

"That's madness!" said Elisha. "You can't have it both ways!"

"Sure you can. Both/and," said Easley with a shrug and a smile.

"But if I'm hearing you *right*, you're saying Jerry should *either* believe what you're saying, *or* he's *wrong*."

"He can believe whatever he wants."

"Then why are you trying to get me to see things your way?" Elijah asked.

Some in the group laughed. Some moaned. Some were sick of the whole discussion. "Let's talk about something else!"

"I'll tell you why!" said Easley, and his usual easy tone grew serious. "Because there's a whole world out there that is plagued by war, starvation, hatred, and bigotry, and some of us feel it just might be worthwhile to help the next generation rise above their petty differences and live in peace and brotherhood. That's what this academy is all about, Jerry and Sally: peace, unity, brotherhood. I believe we can do it. I want all of you to believe it. We've come a long way from the amoeba, folks, and we need to continue the journey as we were meant to do. We need to keep getting better, and then get still better, and then better than that, until we finally get there and we have one, big, peaceful world we can all be proud of." Then he added in a parental, correcting tone, looking straight at Elijah and Elisha. "And all you two are doing is destroying the very things we're about, bringing division, factions, squabbles over words."

It was a stirring speech, and Elijah and Elisha could feel the winds of opinion aligning in Easley's favor. Every other boy and girl eyed them, seeing them as Easley did, as objects of shame and scorn.

Easley's voice softened; he sounded like a preacher giving an altar call. "I think you need to examine your hearts, as all of us are doing, every day, and ask yourselves, what do I really want? To win an argument, or win a friend? To stir up strife, or live in peace? To create factions, or knit together a human family?" He addressed the whole group. "I think it's been a good session. We've been challenged and given a lot to think about. That's it for today."

He started to leave, then paused just long enough to turn and say, "Try sharing something. See how it feels." Then he headed back across the field.

A silence hung over the group like a cold fog. The kids watched Easley for a long, pondering moment before they could finally meet each other's eyes.

Melinda turned to Charlene. "You can share my Walkman."

She nodded and said, "So can you."

Ramon looked through his shirt pocket. "I've got an extra pen if anybody needs it."

Brett called out, "Anybody who wears size 10, I've got a pair of sneakers I don't need."

They all rose from the grass, picking up ties, shoes, and blazers, and having quiet, peacemaking conversations as they walked away.

"Okay, you can use the shower first."

"You can put your books on my side of the floor; it's okay."

"I don't need those pajamas; you can have them."

No one said a word to Elijah or Elisha.

Except for big, strong Alex. He made a special trip over to the cottonwood to give Elijah a rap on the head. "Think you're pretty smart, huh?" Then he said to Elisha, "I'd stay clear of this guy if I were you." He walked away, indulging in one final sneer over his shoulder.

Elisha could see warning signs in her brother's face and hurried over to touch his arm. "Let it go. We don't need any more attention."

He took a deep breath, calmed himself, and nodded.

Nate and Sarah were busily at work in the back of their van, compiling a database, bit by bit.

A photo of Nelson Farmer, the tall, worried-looking rep from the Bureau for Missing Children, came up on Sarah's computer screen. "Nelson Farmer, Senior Director, been with the Bureau for twelve years." She tapped in the print command and the printer started printing Farmer's bio and resume. She wagged her head, stumped. "The guy looks totally clean. Maybe he has delusions of power or something, but he's not masquerading. He really does work there."

Nate sat on the other side, his back to her, tapping at another computer and getting nowhere quick. "The sheriff's offices in Idaho have no record of any lost, wandering kid being found."

Sarah spun around. "Please say again?"

"I've checked with all the north and north central counties. There is simply no record of anyone finding Alvin Rogers and turning him over to authorities."

She rolled her chair around to examine the blank report sheet on Nate's computer screen. "In other words, the file has been erased from the records."

"So no one can go back and find out exactly *where* Alvin was found."

"I don't believe this. How powerful are these people, anyway? They make youth shelters disappear overnight, and now they can hack databases?"

"Well, we both know how easy it is. If these people knew where to look, they could have erased some history, and once the record's gone, it's gone. The first place Alvin shows up as a matter of record is with the Kootenai Medical Center in Coeur d'Alene, right before he was transferred to Harborview. So we do have him popping up in Idaho, but that's all."

There was a loud rap on the passenger door up front, and then it opened.

It was Charlie. "Nate and Sarah!" He clapped, then rubbed his hands together. "We've found somebody!"

They followed Charlie into the dining hall where they met Tyler, an older teen, nineteen to be exact. His life was much more put together since Charlie and Anita had taken him in three years ago. He was now living with an aunt and uncle in Redding, California, and he was planning to start college in the fall.

"Came up here to visit some friends," he told them, "and Charlie and Anita were two of them."

Charlie and Anita beamed with pride and joy as they all sat together at their quiet, corner table. Charlie explained, "We were talking about things, you know? How it's going and what are his plans, and then I asked him about this Knight-Moore Academy thing, and—" He immediately handed it off to Tyler. "Tell Nate and Sarah about that lady you met."

"Her name wasn't Margaret Jones. It was Suzanne Dorning, and she met me on the street down in Phoenix."

"Phoenix!" exclaimed Sarah. "She's been around, if it's the same woman."

Tyler continued, "She invited me to get on a bus and head out for a summer academy where I could earn some high school credits and meet other kids from all over the country. She made it sound great, but I told her no. Something that sounded that good couldn't be on the up and up."

"Don't suppose you can describe her?" Nate asked.

Tyler thought a moment, then shook his head. "It was three years ago. Don't remember that much. She was kind of a red-head, I think. She was young and pretty."

"How do you even remember her name after so long?"

Tyler reached into his coat pocket and pulled out a wrinkled scrap of paper. "She wrote it on the back of the brochure." Nate and Sarah thought their hearts would stop as Tyler slid it across the table. "I stuffed it in my backpack and just left it there. When Charlie asked me about it, I remembered seeing something about an academy and we dug it out."

"Same old backpack!" Charlie wheezed with laughter. "Does God answer prayer or what?"

The brochure was in color, one sheet triple-folded, and looked like it had been left in a backpack for three years. On the front were the words "Knight-Moore Academy." Inside were photographs of a simple campus in a forested setting, classrooms full of bright, cheery students with their hands raised—apparently, all of them had the answer—and catchy claims such as, "Get a head start on your educational future," "Learn as you've never learned before," and "We don't just teach history; we make history!" On the back was Suzanne Dorning's phone number and the address of the academy.

"Let's call the number," said Nate.

"I already did," said Tyler. "It's 'disconnected or no longer in service.'"

"But we have an address," said Sarah, studying the brochure and copying it down. It wasn't much, just the name of the academy followed by Borland, Colorado. "Wonder if Borland, Colorado, is still there?"

"We're about to find out," said Nate.

6

rules and power

The academy offered a class in reading and English, with a choice of morning or afternoon sessions. Well, it was afternoon, and the class turned out to be mandatory, so Elijah signed up for the 3:00 P.M. session. Happily, Elisha had signed up for the same class for the same reasons, and they managed to meet on the walkway fifteen minutes before class started.

"Let's take that bench," Elijah suggested, and they quickly moved to a small, concrete bench in the shade of the library, opening their binders and leafing through their materials for the benefit of anyone watching.

"How're you feeling?" Elijah asked.

"I think I'm finally awake," she replied. "Do you remember the bus ride?"

"No."

"Neither do I."

"I think there was something in that soup we ate."

"I think you're right. I've talked to Marcy and some of the other girls in the dorm. None of them remember the bus ride, either."

Elijah made an effort to look like he was checking his class schedule and not look perturbed. "Doesn't that bother them?"

She could only wag her head and sigh in frustration. "I think it should, but it doesn't. At least they're *acting* like it doesn't. Elijah, it's a fantasyland. Everybody's pretending. There's a weird mind game going on here."

"Tell me about it."

"Do you still have your radio?"

"Yeah."

"I have mine, too, but the headphones are gone."

"Oh, so you're sharing."

"Better keep a close eye on your stuff, what there is of it."

"Uh-huh."

"I want to call Mom and Dad every night, whether they can hear us or not, whether we can hear from them or not. We could trade off each night to save batteries."

"Okay. You want to go first, tonight?"

"Okay." She tried to smile and look like they were chatting about any old thing. "So. What are we going to do?"

"Well, we got into this whole thing to investigate, so there's always that."

"I want to call Mom and Dad every night, whether they can hear us or not, whether we can hear from them or not. . . ."

"Well, yeah, but . . ."

"But where's the back door?"

"Exactly. How do we get out of here if we need to? I haven't seen a road anywhere, and where is this place? They won't tell us."

"We've got to contact Mom and Dad, that's priority *uno*. We need a phone. I'll take a pay phone, a cell phone, anything."

"Haven't seen one. And Bingham said there aren't any."

"There are. These people aren't going to go without phones, even if they expect us to."

Other kids were passing by, making a beeline for class. Elisha checked her watch. "We'd better get to class. Marcy says Mr. Booker is really strict."

———

Mr. Booker's reading and English class convened in a classroom—a neat, well-ordered classroom. The chalkboards were recently washed. The bookshelves were neatly arranged, with all the books grouped by title and with heavy iron bookends holding them in place so not one was lying on its side. There were desks for the girls on the right side of the classroom, desks for the boys on the left side, and down the middle, a perfectly straight aisle. Whitman, Hemingway, Thoreau, and Emerson gazed down from perfectly straight portraits on the walls. There was a certain reserve on the part of the students hurriedly taking their seats; they were talking, but not loudly, and every tie, every blazer, every shoe was present and in place.

Elijah found an empty desk about halfway back—on the left side, of course—and settled in.

Elisha found a desk on the girls' side, front row, on the aisle.

"Hey. Sally, right?"

A young man with bristly black hair and holes in his face where rings and studs used to be was smiling at her.

"That's right," she answered pleasantly. "And you are?"

"Tom Cruise. You know, the movie star?"

She gave him a careful, second look. "*You're* Tom Cruise?"

He tilted his head back and gave her what must have been a Tom Cruise smile. "Pretty impressive, huh?"

"I'm speechless."

"Yeah, just wanted to introduce myself. I'm—"

He was interrupted by a rather rude backhand to his arm.

It was Alex, with tie straight and every wavy blond hair in place, towering over him with a mean gleam in his eye. "I think you're sitting in my desk, bub."

Mr. Cruise said not a word, but gathered his books and went elsewhere.

Alex sank into the desk, very proud of himself.

Elisha was hoping there was a mistake. "That's your desk?"

Alex just sniffed a laugh. "If he can be Tom Cruise, this can be my desk. Call it like you want it." He leaned toward her, giving her a smile she was supposed to like. "So how do you like the place so far?"

She looked him in the eyes. "I'm not sure I've decided. It's different. It's been very interesting."

He gave her a once-over as he said, "Well, let me tell you, it just got more interesting."

Suddenly, a loud, clear, booming voice at the back door startled everyone in the room. "Alex! I believe you're sitting in a desk reserved for Mr. Cruise!"

Alex turned his face forward so he could swear.

Hard heels came marching up the aisle as Elisha looked to see—

"Eyes *forward*, young lady!"

She turned forward and froze there.

Mr. Booker, in burgundy suit, a thick novel under his arm, strode mightily to the front of the class. He was middle-aged and professorial in appearance, right down to the little black reading glasses and receding hairline, but there was nothing weak about him. The way he walked, stood, and glared, this guy was scary, and now he was directing his full attention on Alex, who had the gall to glare right back at him. "You will return to your own desk. Now."

"*This* is my desk, Mr. Booker, sir." Alex had a mocking tone.

The direct challenge made Booker pause, then tilt his head slightly, amused as if by a game. "How? By right of conquest?"

Alex looked around at the other students. "I'm *sharing* it."

That brought a timid laugh from the others that Booker's glare cut short as if he'd used a pair of scissors.

"So that's your truth for today, is it?" Booker asked.

"Hey," said Alex with a haughty grin, "that's how things work around here." He looked at the rest of the class. "Huh? How about it, group? Agreed?"

He saw a whole class, some twenty kids, afraid to express the slightest opinion.

"Well," said Booker, "this does present a problem, doesn't it? You have your truth, and I have mine. Just what are we going to do about that?"

Alex gave an arrogant shrug. "Play 'both/and,' I guess."

"You've been listening to Easley."

Alex just smirked, gave his head a playful, confident little wiggle—

Until Mr. Booker grabbed a fistful of Alex's perfectly combed hair and slammed his head down on the desk. The sound of Alex's skull smacking into the wood made everyone jump.

"Mr. Easley failed to include a vital part of the equation," Mr. Booker growled in Alex's ear as Alex struggled and winced, his face beet red. "*Power*, Alex. *Power*. Something I have, and you don't."

As everyone watched, their hearts pounding, some trembling, Mr. Booker yanked Alex out of his desk—Alex's books and papers went flying—and propelled him down the aisle to a desk

> ... Mr. Booker grabbed a fistful of Alex's perfectly combed hair and slammed his head down on the desk.

halfway back. He didn't wait for Alex to sit there; he *put* him there, and then barked at Tom Cruise, who'd found an empty desk near the back, "Mr. Cruise, you will take your assigned seat, please."

Mr. Cruise leaped, ran, planted his hindquarters in that desk, then sat at attention.

Booker put out his palm toward Alex. "Your tokens. All of them."

Alex, his face red, his eye tearing from being smacked on the desk, his hair still disheveled, dug into his blazer pocket and produced a handful of KM dollars. With obvious resentment, he dropped them into Booker's palm.

Mr. Booker confined Alex to his desk with only a look, then returned to the front of the classroom, his dignity unruffled. "Mr. Cruise, I believe these belong to you." He gave the tokens to Mr. Cruise, then turned, rested against his desk, and surveyed the class, meeting every eye. "Surely there are questions?" There was only silence. He shrugged it off, lightly throwing up his hands. *"Of course. If there is no truth, how can there be questions?"*

His fiery eye fell upon Elisha, who looked back only when she felt him looking at her. "And this is the new student, I presume? Answer me."

"Yes, sir. I'm calling myself Sally."

He took a moment to chuckle at that. "Sally. A nice choice. Are you a movie star? A rock star?"

"No. I'm just Sally."

"Well. First of all, thank you for wearing proper attire. There are those in this class who have had to be reminded—Mr. Jackson! Your collar is up! Thank you, that's better!—who have had to be reminded what ties and blazers are for." He dug a KM dollar from his pocket and set it on her desk. "Now. Sally, since you seem to be such a center of attention, would you please stand and recite."

Elisha hesitated. "Uh, excuse me?"

His eyes narrowed. He repeated slowly, "Stand and recite."

She laughed nervously. "Sir, with all due respect, I just got here. This is my very first day."

His eyes could melt an iceberg. "Sally, I'm hearing an excuse. You know my policy regarding excuses!"

"No sir, I'm sorry. I don't know any of your policies because I've never been here before."

He crossed his arms. "And how would I know that?"

She could come up with only one answer. "Have you ever seen me before?"

He nodded confidently. "Every day."

I'm in fantasyland again, she thought, then said, "That's impossible."

Elisha could sense the silent gasp from the rest of the class.

Booker approached her desk, his eyes threatening. He took back the KM dollar. "You have contradicted me. You do realize that?"

His eyes could melt an iceberg.

She didn't want a debate. She was just trying to find some sense in all this. "Mr. Booker, it would be contradictory for me to say that I've always been here when I've been somewhere else."

"And now you're telling me what to think!"

"I'm just telling you the truth."

"Your *idea* of truth, you mean! But you forget, child, that I might see things another way." His hand went to his desk. His fingers curled around a yardstick. "I might prefer to believe that you have always been here, that you knew good and well what the assignment was, and that you are trying to challenge my authority!" He brought the yardstick around. "You will stand and you will recite." He raised the yardstick, ready to bring it down on her shoulders. "You will stand, or—"

Elijah jumped to his feet so fast his desk dumped over with a horrible clatter. "I'LL RECITE!"

Heads spun around. Eyes—wide, intense eyes—locked on him. Over on the right side of the class, a girl broke into tears.

Time froze. Still holding the yardstick, Booker stood motionless like a still photograph from a scary movie and glared at Elijah. He shot a corrective look and a pointing finger at the girl who was whimpering, and she immediately stifled herself. Finally, he turned and walked down the aisle, his heels loudly marking each step on the hard maple floor. "I did not call on you."

Elijah could look past Booker and see the frightened face of his sister. Nothing would turn him back. "I'll recite, anything you want if I know it, and if I don't know it, you can go ahead and hit me."

Booker raised an eyebrow, impressed. He stole a glance at

Elisha. "You have quite the power to charm, young lady." Then he looked at Elijah and cradled the yardstick in both hands, clearly relishing the thought. "Very well. Recite. But I warn you: Try your very best to please me."

Elijah didn't think he'd be able to look Booker in the eye, but there was something about the words he began to recite that gave him the nerve. "Exodus, chapter twenty: 'You shall have no other gods before me. You shall not make unto thee any graven image, or any likeness of anything that is in the heavens above, or in the earth beneath, or in the waters under the earth. You shall not—'"

"The audacity!" Booker growled and raised the yardstick—

A loud scraping of a desk across the floor! Elisha was on her feet, calling out, "'You shall not take the name of the Lord thy God in vain! Remember the Sabbath day to keep it holy!'"

Now, in front and behind Booker, they spoke in chorus: "'Honor your father and your mother, that your days may be prolonged. You shall not steal. You shall not murder. You shall not commit adultery—'"

"RUBBISH!" Booker roared, looking from one to the other.

There was silence.

"Do you want us to keep going?" Elijah asked.

"NO!" Booker studied both of them, looking back and forth,

"The audacity!" Booker growled and raised the yardstick—

and finally, he lowered the yardstick to his side, tapping it absent-mindedly on the floor as he returned to the front of the room. "That will be quite enough. Please be seated, and I commend you for a remarkable demonstration."

"Thank you—"

"Of rubbish. Pure rubbish." Booker tossed the yardstick on his desk and addressed the class. "Did you notice? Once again, we find ourselves having to confront the same old idea, that somehow, as if from the heavens above, there is Truth, there is Right, there is Wrong." He looked angrily at Elijah and Elisha. "Once again, we have to endure someone putting forth definitive statements of truth!"

"As you have just done, sir," Elijah replied, righting his desk.

He simply laughed that aside. "Oh, yes. You're one of those 'either/or' thinkers, aren't you? Either my truth or yours. Well, I say your Truth is rubbish!" He spread his arms toward the class. "I'm even willing to put it to the group! We are a group, are we not, with the power to agree on what is true? Let me ask you, group: Would any disagree with me?"

No one disagreed. Hardly anyone even looked his direction.

He laughed, basking in victory. "Rubbish!"

The class took turns reading aloud from Hemingway for the rest of the hour. Some read well, were commended, and given KM dollars; some could hardly read at all, were humiliated, and had their dollars taken away. Booker certainly made no friends, but like it or not, it was his hour, his class, his kingdom. He ran things the way he pleased, and though he invited questions— once—no one dared ask any.

When class was finally dismissed and the students were a safe distance away, there were plenty of questions. "Who does he think he is?" "That guy's a psycho!" "I thought classes here were optional! What's this mandatory stuff?" "Man, this place is no fun. It's just like school again!"

Elisha's nerves were frazzled. "Do you think he really would have hit me?"

"He wouldn't have had the chance," Elijah told her.

Elisha just sighed, calming herself. "Well, better day tomorrow."

Warren, a quiet but strong young man with reddish hair and freckles, approached Elisha and Elijah on the sidewalk. "I just want to tell you, you've got nerve, man. I couldn't have faced down Booker like that."

Ramon agreed. "You're one bad dude, Jerry—but I wouldn't let him hit me. I'd cut him up first."

Marcy was crying a little, and touched her forehead to Elisha's shoulder. "I felt so awful for you."

> **Booker certainly made no friends, but like it or not, it was his hour, his class, his kingdom.**

Elisha held Marcy close to comfort her. "It's all right. We just need to learn the ropes, that's all. Tomorrow will go more smoothly."

"What was that?" asked Ramon. "The Ten Commandments?"

"How come you both know the same thing?" asked Warren.

Elijah shrugged. "Doesn't everybody?"

"I've seen the movie," Warren offered.

"Hey," said Ramon, "there goes Booker now."

They all followed his gaze. Mr. Booker, with several teachers and staff, was walking toward the big iron gate that separated the campus from the mansion up in the trees. When he and the others reached the gate, Booker entered a code in the lock and the big gate swung open automatically. As soon as they had all passed through, it swung shut again, and the final, metallic clank could be heard clear across the field.

"Just like prison bars," said Elisha.

"I wouldn't mind a closer look at that place," said Elijah.

"Don't even think about it," said Warren. "Somebody already tried sneaking in there and we haven't seen him since."

Elijah and Elisha each made a point to look normal.

"You mean, one of the guests? One of the kids, like us?" Elisha asked.

"Yeah. He was . . ." He fumbled a bit as if he didn't want to go into it. "Well, just stay away from there and don't worry about it."

"But what do they do in there?" Elijah asked.

"It's academy headquarters. Offices and stuff. I think Mr. Bingham lives up there, and maybe Booker and Mrs. Wendell, the librarian. It's private, that's all. Come on. Let's grab something to eat and then rock out."

———

The Rec Center was a huge pavilion wholly devoted to games, amusement, distraction, and sensory overload, and the doors opened at six o'clock every morning. The video arcade rivaled anything the kids might find in the big city, with row upon row of roaring, thumping, off-road-racing, downhill-skiing, snowboarding, bad-guy-shooting, alien-blasting, fighter-jet-flying, body-bashing machines, flashing, beeping, blurping, exploding, a hot-buttered carnival of glittering lights in the semidarkness, a riotous rumble accented with the loud *clack* of pool balls striking each other and the *bock, bock bobock* of air hockey. Above all this was the pounding, bass-driven throb of rock music from the house sound system—and just below it, the roar of the youthful crowd, all yell-talking to each other in bellows, hollers, and shrieks. Everything that met the eye was overstated, from the comic art and blaring movie posters on the walls to the green, purple, red, and blue neon logos, to the bigger-than-life pictures of television, movie, and rock stars in the halls and restrooms. And all the bodies were in constant motion, silhouettes against the lights, rushing, ambling, bumping, drifting from game to game, machine to machine, group to group, like bees between blossoms.

The kids were in their own clothes now, the clothes they'd

brought on their backs, although there were plenty of Knight-Moore tee shirts, jogging shorts, sweat pants, and other cool sports clothing walking around, available at the Campus Exchange for the right amount of KMs. Now, with different wardrobe choices, the kids could talk with their clothes: Don't mess with me. Don't notice me. I don't care. I'm not different. I'm *really* different. I'm tough. I'm cool. I don't need anybody. I'm available. I'm fat but don't know it. Hey, I don't worry.

Elijah and Elisha decided to split up and mingle, carrying on semi-shouted conversations with anyone who was talkative.

Elijah became the fourth player in a pool game, and managed to jaw with his opponents while they waited for their turn.

"The mansion? That's where all the bigwigs live," a lanky pool shark named Andy told him, chalking his cue. "We got some kids saying weird stuff about it, but ehhh, you don't have to believe everything you hear."

"I heard somebody tried to sneak in there and he never came back," Elijah prompted.

"Yeah, I've heard that."

"No, you didn't," said Roberto, watching his shot drop into the corner pocket. "It's just a bunch of talk."

"A bunch of talk that he didn't hear?" Elijah asked.

"That's right."

"Yeah, he's right, I didn't hear it," said Andy.

Marcy introduced Elisha to some of her friends near the vending machines. Britney and Madonna had heard about Elisha's first day in Booker's class, which immediately gave them a common bond.

"You ask me, that mansion's haunted," said Madonna, leaning on the pop machine as she checked out the boys in the room. "I mean, like, Booker lives up there, so I mean, come on!"

"I wouldn't go up there," said Britney. "One night we heard somebody screaming—I'm not joking! You don't know what Booker and Bingham and all those people might be doing up there."

"Did one kid really go up there?" Elisha asked.

"Yeah, first night we were all here. It was some kind of dare, I think."

"What happened to him?"

"He tried to climb over the wall and he fell inside, and then he screamed, and . . ." She shrugged. "And now he's gone, that's all I know."

"Madonna?"

She just flipped her hair out of her eyes and took a sip from her pop can. "I don't know."

"What don't you know?"

She gave Elisha a puzzled look. "What on earth you're talking about."

"And now he's gone, . . ."

"The kid who went over the wall."

She scowled and shook her head. "Nobody went over the wall."

Elisha looked at Britney, but Britney had already caught a glance from Madonna. "Well, it isn't true anymore," Britney added quickly. "I mean, it happened, but now it didn't. Hey! The Booger game's open!"

"Wanna play?" Madonna asked.

"Sure," said Elisha. "What's the object?"

"What's the object!" Madonna and Britney thought that was funny.

"He got in trouble," said Eric, a wiry little guy who could talk while shooting alien spacecraft out of the sky. He'd been at this one game for over an hour nonstop. "Got in a fight, so Booker and Stern took him up to the mansion, and I guess he got sent home 'cause we never saw him again. Of course, you gotta remember, that's just my truth. That's the way I saw it."

"You saw all this?" Elijah asked, watching spacecraft disintegrate into flaming pixels.

"Just in my own mind. It's not true for everybody. But it's a great story."

"Did you know this guy?"

"Can't say I know anything. Don't know his name, don't know if he even existed—but if he did, I think he was a friend of Alex."

Elisha was just starting to win at the Booger game when someone nudged up close behind her and asked, "How's it going?"

It was Alex. Marcy, Britney, and Madonna turned all giggles.

"All right, I guess," Elisha answered, tapping away at the control buttons, all the more motivated to concentrate on the game.

"Don't worry about what happened today, you know, with Booker," he said. "We're gonna even things up, just you watch."

Elisha, investigating, asked, "And just what did you have in mind?"

"Don't trouble yourself about it. I got other plans for you." He put his big hands on her shoulders and whispered something in her ear.

The Booger game began to flash. In only seconds, Elisha lost all her Kleenex points and the game ended in a giant, green explosion.

"Awwww . . . ," came a chorus behind her.

7

dorm raids

lisha could still hear the dull roar of the games and the heavy thumping of the music from her dorm room. It was after eleven at night. A few of the girls had returned to their rooms, giggling, gossiping, some tired and snippy, but most of the noise was still coming from the Rec Center. Marcy had not returned, and one look at Marcy's totally devastated half of the room told Elisha not to expect her anytime soon. Whoever Marcy was pretending to be, she was definitely not pretending to be anyone organized or disciplined, and one look at the hallway outside said the same thing about the rest of the girls in this building.

It had Elisha worried, not about the messiness, but what it meant and what it could lead to. If trash and clothing scattered about the rooms and hallways and graffiti on the walls didn't matter, what else wouldn't matter? Mrs. Meeks, the dorm supervisor, didn't seem very concerned. She hardly ever came out of her office to check on things.

Elisha reached under her bed and took her radio from its hiding place in the bedspring. Sitting on the bed with her back against the wall, she held the tiny microphone near the corner of her mouth and began transmitting. "Mom and Dad. In case you're within range of this radio . . ." Just talking to Mom and Dad brought a wave of deep longing. "Hi. I miss you." She had to pause a moment and draw some deep breaths. Her voice was still choked when she continued. "Elijah and I are okay. We're trying to find a telephone or any other way to contact you. We've found the Knight-Moore Academy, and from what we've seen, there's no doubt that Alvin Rogers was here." She looked out the window and could see a few dim lights coming from the mansion. "And I think we've found part of the answer to what happened to him."

────────

While Elisha was in her room filing a report, Elijah was taking advantage of the darkness, scouting the big stone wall that enclosed the mansion. He'd already circled the campus looking for a road and found nothing, so the only way in and out of this place had to be through that big iron gate and by way of the mansion. He thought he'd heard some vehicles coming and going up there. A mansion that size had to have a road leading to it, and that road had to go somewhere.

> **Elisha reached under her bed and took her radio from its hiding place in the bedspring.**

He continued along the wall until he came to the right lower corner. From there, the wall continued up the hill, shrouded by thick forest and darkness. He found an opening in the underbrush and pushed his way in. The brush was low and thin and moved aside easily, but the footing was a little tricky. He climbed, step by step, tree by tree.

When he had gained some elevation above the campus, he halted in a small gap in the brush and listened. Tonight's evening of "rocking out" was winding down. The music had stopped. Lights around the campus were blinking out. He was now closer than he'd ever been to the mansion and could see the big, lighted windows through the tangled tree limbs. He shook off a chill. Maybe it was the darkness, or the rumors he'd heard, but that place gave him the creeps.

Then he heard a strange sound below, a yelling, banging commotion.

"Don't these people ever sleep?" he muttered to himself.

Elisha heard the noise, too, only much closer. She jumped out of bed and went to the window. It was too dark to see much, although she could see two or three bodies running around out

She heard a long, loud squeal and footsteps coming down the hall.

there in white KM tee shirts. She heard a long, loud squeal and footsteps coming down the hall. It sounded like Marcy.

BAM! The door opened and it was Marcy, all right, her face red, panting, shrieking and giggling. "It's a raid!" She slammed the door shut, then grabbed a chair to prop against it. "I can't believe it! This is so exciting!"

"Who is it?"

"Alex and all the boys!"

Oh, great! "Where are they?"

"They're raiding the boys' dorm!"

The crash of a breaking window! Angry screams!

"Where's Mrs. Meeks?"

"I don't know!"

"Well, what about Mr. Stern?"

"I don't know."

"Leave the lights off."

━━━━━━

Well, Elijah figured, *with everybody having such a good time down there, I'll never get another opportunity like this one.*

He continued up the hill, keeping the lights of the mansion off his left shoulder, trying to circle it until he found something. So far, he'd found plenty of loose rocks, tangled brush, and low tree limbs, but no break in the forest.

Then he saw something different—very vague in the dark, but different. The amber glow from one of the mansion's yard lights was reaching far back into the forest, suggesting a long, narrow opening, a possible road. He paused a moment to study it.

Then he heard something and quit breathing.

He heard it again. A low, close-to-the-ground snuffing, then a snorting. Some bushes rustled. Some twigs snapped.

Whatever it was, it sounded big.

___

Elisha and Marcy sat in their darkened room, peering out the window through small, cautious cracks in the curtain. There were voices out there, some whooping and hollering, some angry enough to kill. The voices were mostly male, but she could hear some females, too, some laughing, some screaming and swearing. Vague shadows were running in the dark, coming, going, chasing, brawling. Suddenly, startlingly, two raced by just outside the window, one pursuing the other, feet pounding the sod and breath chugging. The one doing the chasing caught up with his quarry, and with a violent jerk, ripping his clothes, dashed him to the ground.

"Okay, okay, I give," came a voice, muffled against the ground.

But blows followed, fist against flesh, and grunts of deep, guttural pain.

Marcy gasped.

Elisha was reviewing in her mind the building exits and escape routes. "We may have to get out of here."

___

Bears are usually afraid of people, so Elijah tried hollering. "YAAA! GO ON! GET OUT OF HERE!"

The thing replied with a deep growl that filled the forest. More branches and twigs were snapping, each sound a little closer. Now he could hear and even feel the heavy thumping of huge feet.

"Guess this one isn't afraid," Elijah considered, but when a huge, furry form came charging his way, he was quite certain. He ran for all he was worth, widening the trail he'd made coming up, breaking out of the woods and into the field with a clear, new insight: "Okay, *one* thing's true around here."

———

Outside the dorm window, the rioting shadows began to retreat into the dark, their time of mischief over. A moment later, except for the soft whimper of a pulverized young man struggling to his feet, it was quiet.

"Is it over?" Marcy asked.

"Looks like it," said Elisha, feeling relieved.

"That was scary."

"Has this happened before?"

"No. Not like this. We've played some jokes on each other, but this was mean." Her frightened eyes widened in the dark and she gave a little gasp. "What if they'd come in here?"

Already, the thought had more than crossed Elisha's mind. "Good question, Marcy. What *if* they'd come in here?"

"They . . . they wouldn't have *done* anything, would they?"

Elisha looked out the window, still afraid she might see shadows lingering and sneaking about. "When there's no right or wrong, why *shouldn't* they do something if they feel like it?"

Marcy had no answer.

Across the field, a tiny light began blinking. A flashlight, most likely, near dorm B. The blinking continued as the light waved back and forth, shining, then obscured behind something, then shining again. There was a pattern to it. Elisha had seen this signal before: the letters E, E, S.

Elijah! He was trying to signal her, using their hailing code, their initials! "Marcy! Do we still have that flashlight?" Every room was issued a flashlight, and now they could put it to good use.

Marcy groped about in the dark until she found their official KM flashlight where she'd left it, on top of the dresser. She joined Elisha at the window, handed her the flashlight, then knelt there, silent and spellbound as Elisha signaled back, ducking the flashlight in and out from behind the curtain to create her signals.

"Who are you talking to?" Marcy asked in a hushed voice. "Is this a code? Where'd you learn to do this?"

"Later," said Elisha.

> "When there's no right or wrong,
> why shouldn't they do something
> if they feel like it?"

Elijah, safe in his room, got her message: "DORM D RAIDED. WE ARE OK. HOW ARE YOU?"

He signaled back, using the curtain to make the flashlight blink. "OK. MAY HAVE FOUND ROAD. STOPPED BY BEAR."

There was a significant hesitation before Elisha answered, "REAL BEAR?"

"REAL BIG BEAR. SCARY."

"STILL NEED BACK DOOR. DAMAGE HERE. FIGHTS."

Elijah could hear Alex and his guys laughing and reliving the raid out in the hall. Freshly stolen KMs were jingling. "TOM CRUISE BEATEN. KMS TAKEN. ALEX WAS LEADER. BE CAREFUL."

"YOU TOO. I MISS MOM AND DAD."

Mom and Dad. Elijah knew he would have missed them anyway, but this place only made their love all the more precious. He signaled back, "WE WILL SEE THEM AGAIN. LETS MAKE THEM PROUD."

"LY." Their code for "Love you."

"LY."

As Elijah put away his flashlight, a chilling thought crossed his mind: *What if we* can't *get out of here?*

Nate and Sarah rented a high-performance, single-engine airplane and flew themselves to Borland, Colorado, in less time than it would have taken to fly commercially. Joe Pike, owner of a local hunting and fishing resort, met them at the airstrip in his SUV.

"I've been checking around," he said as he loaded their gear into the back of his rig. "It's like I told you on the phone. Sure, a lot of people remember the government having some kind of camp or something way up in Cougar Gulch, but that was a few years ago."

"We need to talk to those people," said Nate.

"And we need to see that camp," said Sarah.

An hour later, Pike eased to a stop at the end of an obscure, seldom-used access road. Nate and Sarah climbed out and looked in all directions, enjoying the scenery regardless of their serious mission. This was the great outdoors at its best: green, tree-covered mountains rising steeply on all sides of the valley, their jagged, snow-frosted summits stark against a deep blue, cloud-laced sky; the valley itself, stretched out like a green hammock between the peaks, garnished with young trees, a sparkling stream, and rust-red outcroppings of rock.

"This way," said Pike.

They followed him over a berm of earth that blocked the road and into an open meadow where all the trees were young, only a few feet tall.

Pike stopped. "This is it."

They waited for a clue that he was joking, but it didn't come.

Nate walked several yards into the meadow, looking about. "There used to be a campus here? A whole academy?"

Pike pointed to a mound to their left. "There's some rubble over there, what's left of a foundation." He pointed ahead. "And there used to be a large meeting hall right over there. You can still see the base for the fireplace."

Nate walked far ahead and stooped down to pick up some broken brick from the remains of an old chimney. Carefully scanning the ground, he could see a vague, rectangular shape under the grass, wildflowers, and young trees.

Sarah took out the brochure they'd gotten from the former runaway named Tyler, and compared the photograph on the front with the terrain she was seeing now. The photo couldn't capture all the mountainous background, but it included enough. In the photo, behind a large hall, was the very same rocky outcropping and steep-sided valley she was seeing right now from where she stood.

"What happened to it?" Nate asked. "It couldn't have just rotted away, not in so short a time."

Pike shrugged. "Near as anyone can tell, the government came in and tore it all down, and then they replanted the area. And they did it quick." He surveyed the open field that was once a campus. "Yeah, if you hadn't lived here and hunted here and seen it for yourself, you'd never know there was such a thing."

They returned to Borland, a former mining town trying to

> "What happened to it?" Nate asked.
> "It couldn't have just rotted away,
> not in so short a time."

put on a new face for tourists. There were tackle shops, Joe Pike's Borland Resort, a mine tour, trout ponds, and a tourist center that offered snowmobiling in the winter and river rafting in the summer.

Joe treated them to lunch in his restaurant. "Sure. I can remember busloads of kids coming in for a few weeks at the academy. They'd stop in here for snacks and film and to use the restroom, but after that we never saw them. They'd spend all their time up there."

"And how many years was it here?" Sarah asked between bites of salad.

Joe gave a strange, apologetic look. "Just one."

Both Nate and Sarah had to double-check, leaning over the table toward him. *"Just one?"*

Steve Mackleberg, the owner of the local filling station, shed a little more light on it. "There was a work camp up there for several years, and then the government came in and fixed the whole place up like a YMCA camp. We saw the big yellow buses go by, full of kids, and then two weeks later we saw them all go by again, heading home. I'm not sure what they were doing up there. But you know, you ought to talk to Vicky Johnson, the hairdresser. She and Gus worked up there."

Vicky Johnson, a local lady who did hair, polished nails, and raised trout, talked while she cut a customer's hair in her one-chair beauty shop. "My husband and I got on as assistant care-takers—you know, cutting the grass, sweeping the walks, hauling the garbage, whatever. We worked there for a month to get the place ready for the kids, and then kept it up for the two weeks while the kids were there."

"Just two weeks?" Nate asked.

"And then they said thank you and ran us out of there. We got our paychecks, put a new roof on the house, and the next thing we knew, the academy wasn't there anymore. Your tax dollars at work."

"Where did the kids come from?" Sarah asked, ready to write down the answer.

"Oh, all over the country. I know we had a few kids from Denver. The academy recruited kids in the high schools."

"Um . . . any *particular* schools?"

"Oh, you'd have to talk to—what was her name, anyway? She was the recruiter, in charge of getting kids signed up."

Sarah looked at the back of the brochure again. "Suzanne Dorning?"

"No, no, it was something like Katy or Kathy . . ." With her scissors, she pointed out one of the many photographs and snapshots she had taped to the walls. "Well that's her right there, standing between me and Gus." Sarah and Nate took a close

"Where did the kids come from?"

look. There, standing between her two smiling friends, was a cute, red-haired lady proudly holding up an impressive trout. "Every time somebody catches a trout out of our pond we snap a picture for them to take home. We enjoyed Kathy—that was her name—so we kept a copy."

Sarah gave Nate another second to study the photo, and then looked at him.

"That's her," he said. "That's Margaret Jones."

———

The next night, it was Elijah's turn to make a radio report just in case Mom and Dad were listening. He took his radio from its hiding place under his mattress and recapped the day.

It had been one very tense day. All the darkness and all the stealth of the previous night didn't keep everyone in dorm D from knowing exactly who raided them, whose idea it was, and exactly what was taken. The talk was all over the campus. Alex, the big man of dorm B, and Brett, the big man of dorm D, had been rivals from the beginning, and now they were staring daggers at each other and exchanging vicious little promises.

"Tom Cruise" was trudging around the campus with a puffy face, trying to borrow KMs. Alex and the guys from dorm B kept making little wisecracks about having things that Brett and the guys from dorm D no longer had, and the word *sharing* was floating around like the punch line of a joke. Mr. Easley was laughing about it, confident that everyone had learned a valuable lesson and that, once each person had had time to search his or her heart, the solution to the whole problem would become clear to everyone. Mr. Booker didn't care to hear any whining about it and forbade anyone to talk about it, at least in his class. "This is your world," he said. "You made the bed; you can sleep in it." Mrs. Meeks and Mr. Stern weren't quite as detached; they just handed the whole problem back with the challenge, "This is your world and you know best. See what you can do and we'll back you."

That evening, the music was playing as loud as ever in the recreation center, but half the video games were blurping, beeping, and roaring with no one there to hear them and the pool table was deserted. Most of the kids didn't want to leave their rooms for fear that what little possessions they had would not be there when they returned. The talk had gotten around and everyone expected trouble.

It came. Only moments after Elijah had finished his report and hidden his radio, he heard a loud rapping on his window.

"Elijah! Elijah!" It was his sister.

He cracked the window open. "What are you doing here?"

"You're going to be raided! Brett and a whole gang of kids are on their way over here right now!"

Elijah heard a terrible crash at the end of the hall. "I think they've arrived."

"Don't let them find your radio!"

"Don't worry."

"I'm going to get somebody in charge. We can't let this go on."

"Go for it."

"What are you going to do?"

"I don't know—see if I can keep anybody from getting killed, I guess."

He could already hear a terrible tumult in the hallway. He quickly stepped outside his door, closed it behind him, and stood there, overwhelmed.

There were no fun and games out here. A mob of guys, maybe two dozen strong, were muscling their way into the rooms, getting shoved back by the occupants, kicking the occupants. Two guys trying to push their way into room 13 were rammed backward by a chair in their gut, then tripped over two other guys wrestling and slugging on the floor. Alex was in the hall, taking on all comers with what appeared to be a chair leg. A drawer from a dresser came flying out of room 9, tumbling and spilling shirts and socks on the floor. Brett and a hulking buddy burst from room 10, bellowing in triumph as they stuffed KMs in their pockets, and immediately began trying to shove their way into room 8, right next door to Elijah. It was all happening so fast, so noisily. There were so many bodies running everywhere, banging, throwing, shoving, kicking, hitting. The hallway was filling with drawers, clothing, shoes, bars of soap, towels, anything that could be tossed, trashed, or spilled just to rile the owner. Another chair came flying into the hall, then three drawers, and then a mattress. By now there might have been five all-out fistfights going on, but the fighters were changing opponents so often it was hard to keep track.

Three of Elijah's neighbors, from rooms 3, 4, and 5, were now in the hallway, visibly frightened as they stood near their doors watching a wave of violence come their way.

Elijah knew what to do in their case. He spread his arms toward them like a cop doing crowd control. "Guys, get out of here. It isn't worth it."

Shawn, a meek and mixed-up kid severely lacking in muscle, took Elijah's advice and fled out the far door. Jim, big enough to hold his own but too timid to try it, followed him. That left Warren, the neighborly kid Elijah'd gotten to know. Warren was angry, and stood his ground. "They're not taking my stuff."

Elijah turned just in time to see three guys coming their way, ready to challenge that. "Warren, it isn't worth it."

The guy in front, an obvious scrapper with a missing tooth and a face full of pimples, looked at Warren and announced, "Hey, I like those pants!"

It took only microseconds for Elijah to think it through: three against one; if Warren runs, they'll chase him and get what they want. Three against two? Well, at least the odds were better.

"It's worth it," he concluded, and stepped into their path.

8

crusades and inquisitions

Elisha was furious as she stormed across the field toward her own dorm building, rehearsing in her mind what argument—or wrestling hold—she would use to get that stupid, inept, irresponsible wimp-of-a-woman Mrs. Meeks to get off her relativistic rump and *do* something about all this! Whether Meeks was in her room or anywhere else, Elisha was going to find her, and no matter what cutesy, feel-good, we-are-the-world, global village glop Meeks might use to excuse all this nonsense, Elisha was going to get some action!

Then Marcy came galloping by, screaming and giggling along with some other girls, including Charlene and Melinda. There was no question they were making a beeline for the trouble, and that instantly changed Elisha's plans. She did a 180 and headed back. "Marcy! Marcy, don't!"

The girls didn't even turn around.

Dorm A had become a battleground just like dorm B, only a few octaves higher. The hallway was a blizzard of clothing, pillows, combs, makeup, *everything* flying everywhere, including the frequent flash and tinkle of pilfered KMs. There were slap-clashes, tugs-of-war, shrieks, cursings, screams, and threats; girls were scratching, biting, kicking, pulling hair. Elisha went into the melee only deep enough to grab a fistful of Marcy's blouse and yank her out the door. "How *dare* you! Are you out of your mind?"

Marcy was indignant over the interruption. "What's your problem?"

"What's my problem? Don't you remember last night, how scary that was, how scared we were? Don't you remember saying 'Ooo, what if they'd come in here?'"

Marcy's eyes seemed totally blank. "So?"

Elisha wanted to slap her. "So kids got *hurt* last night! And they're getting hurt tonight! Stealing things and wrecking things, and fighting, it's wrong!"

"No, it isn't. We're just getting back at them."

Just then, Melinda came running out the door with a brand-new Walkman in her hand. "Hey, Cher, you're missing out!"

Again, Elisha was incredulous. "Melinda! What are you doing? You can't take that!"

"Sure I can. I want it."

Elisha was trying to believe that a brain cell, just one tiny brain cell, might still be working behind those dead-as-a-dolly, baby blue eyes. "Melinda, aren't you the one who was all upset because somebody stole your Walkman? Don't you remember how it felt to be ripped off?"

"I feel good now," Melinda answered.

"We're just having fun," said Marcy. "It isn't wrong if we're having fun."

"It isn't wrong," Melinda said flatly. "Come on, Cher."

"Cher?" Elisha questioned.

"I got tired of Marcy," said Elisha's roommate as Melinda pulled her back inside.

"Had enough?"

Elijah wanted to show mercy to the big guy with pimples and the missing tooth, but from a safe distance. Standing several feet away, he stretched out his hand as a token of friendship.

The big guy was still on the floor, half doubled over from having his wind knocked out. He and his buddies were able to throw a few good punches before—

He looked around. Where *were* his buddies?

"They're gone," said Elijah. "They're okay—at least, they were walking."

The big guy's back pain and abdominal discomfort gradually gave way to embarrassment and wonder. He remembered grabbing Elijah with every intention of putting his head through the plaster, but whatever happened between that moment and the moment his own body slammed into the floor was a stomach-turning blur.

"What's your name?" Elijah asked.

"Rory."

"I'm calling myself Jerry. This here is Warren."

Elijah was still offering his hand. Rory took it, and Elijah helped him to his feet.

"You're good," Rory said, rubbing his bruised shoulder.

"You're pretty good yourself," said Elijah.

The big raid was over. Brett and his whole gang had done enough damage and received plenty, and now they were gone. Alex and the men of dorm B were picking themselves up, gathering up their scattered belongings, and counting what items weren't there anymore. Some of them were cheering, apparently winners in the brawl, but overall, the mood was sour.

Elijah spoke as a friend to Rory as he eyed his still-rowdy, still-angry dorm mates. "You'd better get out of here."

Rory hurried out the far door.

As soon as the door closed behind the last invader, Warren let out a whoop. "Wooo! Did we whip their butts or what?"

Elijah wasn't cheering. "Warren, take a look around. We don't want to make this a habit."

The next day, Elijah skipped lunch, choosing to spend some time sitting alone on the grass behind the library, scribbling away on a class assignment. Not far from him, a lonely fence post cast a short, noonday shadow on a dry, bare patch of ground. Every few minutes, with an eye on his watch, he took a small twig and poked it in the ground, marking the very tip of the post's shadow. After a half-hour, a single file of twigs traced a gradual arc across the ground as the shadow moved sideways and also grew shorter. Elijah started checking the time every minute, then every thirty seconds as he watched the shadow. As the shadow passed through its shortest length—high noon—he checked the time repeatedly and wrote it down. "7:42 and 15 seconds . . . 7:42 and 30 seconds . . ." He kept marking the time until the shadow began to lengthen again, then went back to the twig that marked the shortest shadow and from that, he determined the time the shadow had passed that point. "7:43 and 12 seconds, Greenwich Mean Time. All right!"

———

Then, back to the unreal world. At 1:30—or thereabouts—Mr. Easley kept wearing that smile as he addressed a group of scowling, bruised, scratched, and torn students. The dress code was still casual, but today some of the kids weren't wearing a complete uniform because they no longer had one. There were bumps on some of the heads, scratches and bruises on some of the faces, a puffy eye here, a split lip there. Apart from a small number of neutrals who found it best to sit somewhere in the middle, the whole group was clearly divided: the A and B dorms on Easley's left and the C and D dorms on his right—and sitting prominently on each side, eyeing each other like two roosters in the same chicken yard, were Alex and Brett.

Oh, you could feel the tension.

"We're actually getting better and better," said Easley. "Did you know that? As we keep evolving from generation to generation, our capacity for good, our ability to solve our own problems, just keeps improving, and we need to be a part of that. We need to pitch in for peace."

No one applauded, but Elijah did raise a hand. "Why? What's wrong with war?"

Alex suddenly came to life. "Yeah. What's wrong with war? I'd like to have a little war right now!" He shot a dirty look at Brett.

"Anytime you're ready," said Brett, returning fire.

The two sides exploded in shots and countershots. "And I want my stuff back, right now!" "It's mine now!" "Just wait 'til tonight!" "You don't scare me!"

It took Easley several minutes and overworking that smile to get things quiet again. "Listen. War is exactly what we're trying to avoid, and Jerry, I don't appreciate your even bringing up the subject."

"I didn't bring it up. It's here, right in our faces, and I think you should deal with it."

"We all have our own beliefs—"

By this time, Elijah was running out of patience and getting visibly, red-facedly angry. "I want you to tell us that fighting and stealing are wrong. Can you do that?"

Easley looked across the group. "What does the group think?"

"Bring it on," said Alex, hitting his palm with his fist.

"Oh, yeah," said Brett.

More hollering, more threats, more dirty looks. If there hadn't been at least a few kids wanting peace, and if Easley hadn't taken a position between them, the whole discussion time might have ended in a riot right there. "Easy, now! Take it easy!" he said.

"Looks like the majority thinks fighting and stealing are okay," said Elijah.

"Except for one thing," said Easley, addressing all of them. "Respect."

Alex thought that was funny. *"Respect?"*

Both sides moaned with disgust and mockery as they eyed each other.

"Respect," Easley repeated. "Listen, our world is full of different cultures, different views of right and wrong, and we're seeing an example of that right here. But we don't have to believe the same things, we don't have to agree with anyone else's idea of right and wrong as long as we simply respect each other. If respect is there, then we have enough good within ourselves to rise above our differences."

Elisha piped up, "Mr. Easley, in some cultures, they love their neighbor. In some cultures, they *eat* their neighbor. Which do you respect?"

"I respect them both."

"Both/and," Elijah muttered in disgust.

"You can't have it both ways," Elisha said, actually scolding him. "If you respect my neighbor's right to invade my room and take my things, then you sure don't respect my right to peace and safety!"

"Either/or," said Elijah.

Easley came back, "Every person has a right—"

"No!" said Elisha. "No one has the right to do something that's wrong!"

Easley leaned toward her. "And I suppose *you're* going to tell us what's right and wrong?"

Some of the group murmured, "Yeah, who do you think you are?" "Yeah, who gave you the right?"

"I don't decide what's right and what's wrong," Elisha answered. "God decides."

The moans and hoots from the group were so loud they echoed back from the buildings across the field.

Elisha pressed on, completing her thought for the whole group. "Remember the Ten Commandments? Well, there are two more we didn't get to recite in Booker's class: Don't lie, and don't want something that belongs to someone else. I think those two commandments right there would solve a lot of the problems around here."

Now Easley leaned back, smiling, obviously glad Elisha had said such a thing. "Ah. God. Religion. Holier-than-thou. Thou shalt not. Is that how it works? Just impose your religion on everyone so they can't think for themselves?"

"It isn't like that. God gave us—"

"Set yourself up as the one who makes all the rules, and tell everybody they have to see things your way because, after all,

> Easley leaned toward her.
> "And I suppose you're going to
> tell us what's right and wrong?"

you have God in your camp. Now you have all the rights: the right to criticize and persecute and condemn, and why not lead a few more Crusades and Inquisitions while you're at it?"

"He twisted everything we said," Elisha lamented as she and Elijah walked across the field together.

"He's good with speeches, have you noticed? When things start getting too illogical for him to argue, he starts working on everyone's feelings so nobody's thinking anymore."

"And now we're the intolerant bigots and know-it-alls."

"And nobody's really thought everything through. Very handy."

"And very dangerous. Elijah, I'm all for investigating, but we're losing what friends we may have had, and I don't know what's going to keep these kids from doing . . . something worse."

A voice called from behind them, "Hey! Jerry!"

Oh-oh. It was Rory, the big guy from last night. *Oh, please, Lord, don't let him be looking for a fight.* Elijah tried to keep his face from showing what he was thinking.

Rory didn't stop to talk, but just passed by as he handed Elijah a note. "Somebody wants to talk to you." He kept going without looking back.

"Well, I'm glad *somebody* does," Elisha complained.

Elijah read the note. "It's from Mr. Booker."

144

The note, in Booker's handwriting, included a rough map showing Elijah where to find the plain, unmarked door in back of the
office building. Elijah reported to that door immediately and
gave it a gentle knock.

"Come in," came Booker's voice from inside.

Elijah opened the door and stepped into a small tool room.
There were garden tools—shovels, rakes, hoes, picks, axes—
hanging on the walls, a wheelbarrow, some sacks of fertilizer, and
a small workbench with some hammers, screwdrivers, and a vise.
Mr. Booker was standing there, an elbow on the workbench,
looking at him. He seemed entirely out of place in here. Elijah
remained by the door and left it ajar.

"Come in, Jerry, and close the door."

"Why am I here, Mr. Booker?"

Booker smiled understandingly. "No need for concern, Jerry. This
meeting is off the record and totally nonthreatening, I assure you."

Elijah found a rake and let the handle drop through the gap
in the door, preventing it from closing. Then he remained where
he was. "Go ahead."

With a resigned smile, Booker began. "So you've gotten to
know Rory."

"Not the way I'd like to."

Elijah remained by the door
and left it ajar.

"Well, it was Rory who recommended you. He was very impressed with your martial arts skills last night."

"Recommended me for what?"

Booker tried to look relaxed, propping one foot on the fertilizer sacks. "You're a bright fellow, a clear thinker, not flighty. A good student, too. Very resourceful, and even courageous. I've been giving it some thought, and I've decided to offer you a very special privilege.

"As you've observed, things are getting out of hand: the raids, the violence, the looting, and I'm sure plenty of other things we have yet to discover. Jerry, I'm sure you understand, when any society is threatened with disorder, firm measures must be taken. The evil has to be contained."

"I thought you didn't believe in evil."

He chuckled. "It's just a convenient term I'm using for, shall we say, disruptive, undesirable behavior? When people can't be trusted to control their behavior, then someone else has to do the controlling. That's what police departments are for; security guards; metal detectors. Well, I am in need of policemen. I need to know what the kids are thinking, what trouble might be brewing so it can be dealt with. I may even need some brute force to contain disruptions."

"So you want me to be a cop?"

"Mm-hm."

"And a . . . an informant?"

Booker weighed Elijah's choice of words and finally agreed with a nod. "But I have no illusions. Loyalty comes at a price, like anything else." He reached into his blazer pocket, pulled out his wallet, and produced two twenty-dollar bills, laying them on the workbench. "Would it be worth, perhaps, forty dollars—forty *real* dollars—per day, plus a pipeline to all the KMs you might need? I can also see to it that other privileges make themselves available."

"And who would I be working for? You?"

"For me, and indirectly, the academy. You won't be alone, of course. I've already hired some others among the student body, Rory being one of them."

"To be what? Hired thugs?"

He laughed. "Well, you make it sound so sinister. But think of the advantages, the main one being order on the campus. No more terrible disruptions, no more lootings, no more injuries." He looked at Elijah a moment, and then raised an eyebrow as he said in a softer voice, "And the advantage for you personally."

"Which is?"

"You would be connected with someone in power. I can make things happen. I can change the game to your advantage." He leaned closer to Elijah, exhilarated with his own sales pitch. "You've seen me and the others pass through that gate every evening. My boy, inside that gate is where the power is."

Elijah paraphrased one of Booker's pet slogans. "It's all about power, and you have it."

"Exactly."

Elijah ran his teeth over his lower lip and then said, "You're really scary, you know that?"

Booker seemed flattered. "Fear works."

"Especially if you have spies and head-breakers working for you."

"A good general must have an army."

"The same goes for an emperor, or a dictator, or a führer. That's the scary part. What you're after is control, am I right? You're trying to contain evil."

"Admittedly."

"But if you don't believe in truth, or right and wrong, then who's going to contain *you*?" He put his hand on the doorknob.

"*Eighty* dollars a day!" Booker dug out two more twenties.

Elijah shook his head in wonder. "Mr. Booker, it's like you and I are from different planets or something. For you, it's all power and money. For me, it's God. It's Truth. I could never work for you. But thanks for your consideration."

He went out the door, politely closing it after him.

Elijah and Elisha showed up for Mr. Booker's afternoon class several minutes early—not that they were eager to get there; they just didn't want to risk being late. They'd already had one face-to-face with him, and now, after that little meeting in the tool room, there couldn't be much goodwill left between them.

BAM! The door burst open right at the top of the hour and Booker entered the room. All eyes went forward. The sudden hush announced him as loudly as any trumpet fanfare.

"Pass your homework to the front!"

One-page assignments were passed forward, desk to desk, to the front. Elisha received the pages from her row, stacking them neatly in front of her. How some of these kids found the time to write anything was a bit of a mystery. One look at the stack told her some didn't.

"Give them here," Booker ordered, and all the front-row students handed them over. Booker took them in hand without looking at them. His eyes were doing a slow sweep of the class, ray-gunning every kid one at a time.

Elijah could see most of the class from where he sat, and knew what Mr. Booker was noticing. *Oh, boy*, he thought, *here it comes*.

After a long, chilling moment, Booker crossed his arms and announced in a very dark tone, "You can be certain that you have made a very grave mistake."

Heads pivoted about. Guilt was everywhere.

"Tonya! Where is your *white* blouse?"

Tonya was wearing a ragged denim shirt under her burgundy blazer. "Stolen, sir."

"Samuel? Your white shirt and your tie?"

"Stolen."

"Stolen, *sir*," Booker barked.

"Sir," Samuel replied.

"Marvin! You aren't even wearing your *shoes*!"

"Uh . . . can't find 'em, sir."

Booker scanned the room one more time. Out of some

149

twenty-plus students, only six or seven had a complete uniform. The rest were wearing whatever pieces they had left, horribly mismatched with street clothes. By God's grace, Marcy—oh, her name was *Cher* now—and Elisha had avoided the first raid, so they still looked sharp. Elijah and Warren had complete uniforms, but only because they'd decked Rory and his two buddies before they could loot their rooms. Brett's wardrobe was apparently unscathed.

"Where is Alex?" Booker asked.

For a moment, there was no answer.

Then Brett spoke up. "Sir, I heard Alex say he was going to get some sleep." Then he added, "He, uh, he said he needed sleep more than he needed your class."

Booker raised an eyebrow, leaning back against his desk, sufficiently, theatrically offended. "Rory. Tom. Jamal. Clay. Bring Alex here, place him in his desk, and make sure he stays there. Oh! And make sure he brings all his KMs with him."

Four big guys rose from their desks. Elijah knew Rory, Tom, and Jamal—they'd met under last night's unfortunate circumstances. They were big, tough, and ugly. Clay, the fourth guy, looked even worse. None of them were wearing a complete uniform, but Booker didn't seem to notice. Elijah could guess: Each had had his own little meeting with Booker in the tool room, and now Booker was "changing the game to their advantage." They left the room with gleeful, hungry looks on their faces.

Brett was looking a little gleeful himself. The first three guys *were* from his dorm, weren't they? But what about Clay? He was supposed to be one of Alex's buddies. Forty bucks a day must have looked pretty sweet.

Booker went on with business. "Tonya, you will be fined five KMs, as of right now."

She was devastated. "But—"

"NOW!"

She dug in her pocket and produced five coins. "It's not my fault. . . ."

"I heard an excuse. Two more. Samuel! Five KMs for the missing shirt, five for the missing tie! And Marvin! Five for each missing shoe!"

It took a lot of class time to collect fines from so many law-breakers, but this was Booker's way. He seemed to enjoy punishing people as much as teaching them. The KMs jingled into Booker's wooden "penalty bowl" like doubloons into a pirate's treasure chest.

"You will replace whatever you are missing by purchasing it at the Campus Exchange, using, of course, your KMs." He gave the penalty bowl a knowing look as he added, "If you have no KMs, the cafeteria will issue a ten KM credit for skipping a meal."

The kids would have moaned, but that would have cost them.

"And, of course, you will abandon all thoughts of protest or appealing to fairness. I require uniforms and I exact penalties because I rule your lives. Period. Are there any questions?"

The room was silent.

"Of course not."

Then Rory, Tom, Jamal, and Clay returned, bursting through the door with Alex walking—sometimes—between them, some bruises on his face and some blood on his forearm. He wasn't dressed for class. As a matter of fact, he was hardly dressed at all, wearing only a tee shirt and jogging shorts. The four big bruisers dropped him in his desk and then stood there, defying him to get up. He'd learned better than that and chose not to, but sat there glowering, huffing through clenched teeth, holding the wound on his arm.

Booker saw the blood and tossed a box of tissues to Rory, who gave them to Alex. Alex dabbed the wound but didn't say thank you.

"Things got a little rough. He hit the corner of a table," Rory explained.

Booker extended his open palm, and Rory tossed him Alex's bag of KMs. The bag was full and heavy, landing in Booker's hand with an audible *chink!* "You will never avoid my class again. *None* of you will avoid my class—ever!"

Alex's voice was hissing, almost weeping, with anger. "Who are you to tell me what to do?"

"ARE YOU BLIND!?" Booker's voice was so loud, so intimidating, that everyone in the room flinched. "You have just experienced the answer to your question, Alex! How many different ways must I demonstrate it?"

Booker tossed the bag of KMs back to Rory. "Divide it amongst yourselves."

As Alex watched his KMs counted out and tossed from hand to hand right over his head, he nearly spit the words at Clay, "You traitor!"

Clay only shrugged and jingled the coins around in his hand.

A chuckle from across the room turned Alex's head.

It was Brett, smiling, gloating, in full uniform, nice and neat, enjoying every moment. He even produced an extra tie from his pocket. "Missing something?"

"You think it's over?" Alex asked him.

Brett just wagged his head slowly. He knew where Alex was going.

"You and me," said Alex.

"Anytime, anywhere," said Brett.

Booker stood there listening, observing. "We appear to have some ongoing, irresolvable issues here."

Just then, the door opened, and Mr. Easley stuck his head in. "Excuse me, Mr. Booker. Don't mean to interrupt. I was wondering—"

Booker was jubilant. "Mr. Easley! Just the man we need!" He indicated the two seething combatants. "We have two kings here, two nations at war. Perhaps you can help them resolve their differences without killing each other."

Easley eyed the two boys knowingly and said, "I guess it's about that time, isn't it?"

"You may as well take them off my hands, Mr. Easley. Take them all. They're useless to me today."

Easley took charge. "Okay, everyone. Let's gather outside, on the fifty-yard line. Form a wide circle and wait 'til I get there. Brett, better swing by your room and get out of that suit. Let's go."

The class rose hurriedly to their feet.

"This is gonna be *good!*" said Clay.

9

the student king

T hey moved into the field, scattered clusters of concern and anticipation, whispering, bantering, wondering.

"What's happening?"

"You mean they're going to fight?"

"You think Brett can take this guy?"

"You're the man, Alex."

"Does this mean we get our stuff back?"

"Where do we go?"

"The football field, fifty-yard line."

Mr. Easley arrived in time to direct traffic. "Okay, back up, back up. Form a circle. Back up a little more, make some room so everyone can see. Alex, you stand over on this side." Brett arrived, in jogging shorts and tee shirt, ready. "Okay, come over here; Brett, you and your group stand over on that side."

Mr. Easley was carrying two pairs of boxing gloves. He handed one pair to Alex, one pair to Brett.

The smirk on Alex's face just stayed there as he clustered with his closest buddies from dorm B and put on the gloves. Brett maintained a stony face, continually sizing up his opponent, as Rory and Jamal tied his glove laces. All around the circle, guys were muttering, bragging, placing bets; girls were bickering, giggling, scolding, choosing sides. Elijah and Elisha just tried to appear as neutral as possible. They didn't care at all who won; they didn't want to see this ridiculous fight in the first place.

"Okay, everybody, listen up," said Easley, standing in the center of the circle. "I want you all to understand, you're looking at two different realities, two different ways of seeing things, and it's very normal. It's the way history has always flowed and mankind has always evolved from one way of thinking to a better way of thinking. This is one way we keep getting better and better." He beckoned to Alex and Brett, bringing them into the center of the circle where they faced each other like two heavyweights before a bout. "There isn't going to be a winner or a loser. This isn't going to be one man's viewpoint prevailing over the other man's viewpoint. It's going to be the melting together of two viewpoints to form a new one. After today, we're all going to see things differently, and we're going to have peace, so keep that in mind during this process." He stepped back. "Okay. Let's go."

Alex and Brett approached each other, gloves raised, circling, eyes mean. The crowd began to holler, cheer, shriek. Alex threw the first punch, and it landed squarely in Brett's face. He stumbled backward. Half the crowd cheered, half jeered. Brett stepped in again, got punched again, but landed one himself. They went toe-to-toe, no strategy, no skill, just a brawl. Alex connected with Brett's face again, then sent a haymaker into Brett's stomach. Brett doubled over, lost his balance, and fell.

Easley motioned Alex back, motioned for quiet, then spoke to Brett, loudly enough for everyone to hear. "Brett, have you thought about how you'd like to end this?"

Brett was furious, stumbling to his feet. "By caving his face in!"

"Come on and do it," said Alex, waving him on.

Easley stepped back and let them go at it again.

Alex was simply a better fighter. Brett went down again, this time with a nosebleed.

Easley stepped in again, this time with a suggestion. "What about all the stuff you took from dorm B? Maybe you could reach an agreement of some kind."

Brett only pushed Easley away as blood ran down his face. "What about all the stuff *they* took?"

Easley looked to Alex for a reply.

Alex just smirked, as usual. "You want it, come and get it."

Easley stepped back and let Brett charge.

Brett did land a few punches, mainly to Alex's body, and mainly because Alex let him. Then Alex chose his moment and hammered Brett's head with a volley of punches, sending him to the ground a bleeding, dazed mess.

"Get up!" someone yelled.

"Don't get up!" yelled others.

They went toe-to-toe, no strategy, no skill, just a brawl.

Brett was trying to get up, but he had neither strength nor balance and rose repeatedly only to crumble to the ground again.

Easley approached Alex this time. "Alex, perhaps you'd like to offer some terms of surrender?"

Alex approached Brett, standing over him like a conqueror. "You give us back all our stuff—starting with my tie."

"You could make it work both ways," Easley suggested. "Everybody give everything back, but let Alex be the king. He's earned it."

Alex liked that a lot. Half the crowd was undecided.

Brett couldn't decide, either, but silently wiped blood from his face with the back of his glove.

Easley put a hand on Alex's shoulder. "You can be a benevolent king. Think of it. With one ruler, one boss in charge, everybody can live by the rules you make; and you can make sure we're all safe and cared for." He turned to the crowd surrounding them. "How about it? We could join together under one new viewpoint and have one big family. No more raids, no more fights, just one big, peaceful world."

The kids picked up on that idea quickly. "Yeah! One family!" "King Alex!" "We can get our stuff back!" "No more raids! Cool!"

Easley spoke to Alex, knowing Brett would hear him. "And Brett could be your lieutenant. He was pretty brave to take you on. I know he could serve you well. Couldn't you, Brett?"

Brett propped himself up on his elbows and looked to the crowd all around him.

"One world!" they cheered. "One world! One world!"

Brett looked up at Alex, searching his face.

Alex dropped the smirk and actually looked kind. "Hey. You give me respect, then I'll respect you and we'll put everything back together. You get your stuff, we get ours, we stand together. Sound good?"

Brett thought, listened to the crowd, and finally smiled concedingly. "Okay."

Alex helped Brett to his feet, and with their arms around each other's shoulders, they raised their free hands to the crowd.

The cheer from the kids echoed across the campus. The war was over. They were getting better and better.

Alex winked at Elisha. She smiled politely.

He smiled gloatingly at Elijah. Elijah tried to smile but couldn't find a reason to do so.

⸻

Ms. Jennifer Whitman, principal of Smithson High School in Denver, had met Kathy Simons. "She's one little ball of energy, let me tell you! I think she covered just about every high school in greater Denver."

"What did she do?" Sarah asked.

"She was a recruiter. She presented the program to us, we recommended some candidates, and then she did the final screening. Three of our kids qualified, so we're proud of that."

"So what can you tell us about the academy?" asked Nate. "We have two kids who are interested."

Ms. Whitman gave them a consoling look. "I hate to be the bearer of bad news, but I think the program's been discontinued."

Sarah didn't have to pretend surprise. "Really?"

"The government gave it a test run, I guess, and decided to scrap it. That's a shame because I think it was definitely time for such a project."

"Well, what was it?" Nate asked.

Ms. Whitman reached into a desk drawer and pulled out three brochures, all similar in size and style, but different in one strange way: The photographs in each brochure were of a different academy; different buildings, different setting, and different address on the back. "The Knight-Moore Academy was a two-week program offered for four summers in four different locations around the country. We got involved in the academy held in Borland three years ago. It wasn't for everybody. It was experimental, and all the students went into it fully aware of that."

"What kind of experiment?" Sarah asked.

"A team of educators wanted to explore new techniques in education from a global perspective, and I think it worked. The kids came back with a wider, fresher, well, *global* understanding. I think they came to realize that there is definitely more than one way to look at things. There are many different truths out there."

Nate read the different locations on the brochures. "So there was one in Illinois two years ago, one in Virginia a year ago, and the one in Colorado three years ago."

"And the very first one was, I believe, in Southern California. I don't have any information about that."

"Could we make some photocopies of these brochures?" Nate asked.

"Certainly."

"And, uh, you don't have any current address or phone number for Kathy Simons, do you?"

"Just the information on the back of the brochure."

As they drove back to the airport in their rented car, Nate spouted a question bothering him. "If the Knight-Moore Academy is a government project, why doesn't Morgan know about it? Why doesn't the president know about it?"

Sarah leafed through the photocopies of the brochures. "So far we've seen a youth shelter and an entire campus disappear. What if these other campuses aren't there anymore?"

"We'd better hope they are." She looked at him for a further explanation, and he responded, "Because if they aren't there anymore, then wherever the kids were taken . . ."

"Okay. No need to say it." She sorted through the photocopies and the scanned photograph of the mysterious redhead. "I'll fax all this stuff to Morgan."

The music from the Rec Center could be heard anywhere on campus. Elijah could hear the thumping bass notes even from behind the library, where he'd returned to his secluded little spot by the lonely fence post. This time, he had a length of thread he'd pulled painstakingly from the edge of his bedsheet, his official

KM flashlight, and a small, six-foot tape measure he'd purchased at the Campus Exchange.

It was a clear, beautiful night. The stars were out. Perfect. He immediately found the Big Dipper and, from there, the North Star. Now all he had to do was use the post, the thread, and the tape measure to answer the big question of the evening: Exactly how high in the sky, in degrees, was the North Star?

The Rec Center was hopping again. Everyone was back, feeling safe, having a great time, and actually celebrating having a Student King on Campus. In the lounge area near the vending machines, Alex sat on a picnic table, presiding over the restoration of all stolen—or rather, *shared*—goods, wearing his recently recovered tie around his head like a victor's wreath, a token of the new peace accord. Tonya had her blouse again, Samuel had his white shirt and tie, and Marvin had just received his shoes. Melinda was moping a bit; she'd returned the Walkman she'd taken, but was still "sharing" a Walkman with Charlene, who didn't respect her very much.

Mr. Easley happened to be there that night, smiling as broadly as ever, patting backs and giving hugs. "I think it's going to work."

"We're getting better and better," said Britney, groping in her pockets. She turned to Madonna. "Can I borrow a KM?"

"Get your own," said Madonna, in a mood.

"C'mon, I want to buy a Coke."

"Yeah, and maybe I'm tired of you mooching all my KMs. Try earning a few."

Easley overheard them and called out, "Hey, we're celebrating!" They only pouted at him.

"Okay, tell you what." He went to the pop machine, used a key from his pocket, and swung the machine open. "Nobody owns this pop, anyway. We have all things in common. Let's pass the drinks around and celebrate our new unity!"

Now, that drew a crowd! A happy riot gathered instantly and the machine was empty in a matter of minutes.

Alex held his pop can high. "Three cheers for Mr. Easley! Hip hip!"

They all hoorayed the three cheers, cans high in the air.

Easley waved to them all. "Gotta go. Have fun." He went out the door as they cheered after him.

"Better and better!" Cher, formerly Marcy, cheered, holding her pop can high.

Elisha, sitting on the bench next to Cher, looked glumly at her can of pop and just shook her head.

"*Now* what's the matter?" Cher asked.

"Better and better. I get so sick of hearing that."

"What's the matter with better and better?"

"You're not thinking, Marcy—I mean, Cher. If there's no truth, then how can we know we're getting better? Better than what? How can we know the difference?"

"It *feels* better."

"Just like 'Cher' feels better than 'Marcy.' But can't you see? Both those names are a fantasy. This whole place, this whole *thing* is just one big lie."

Cher thought about that only a moment, then asked, "So who are *you* really?"

"Sally!" Alex called from his perch on the picnic table. "Hey, Sally!"

Elisha didn't realize he was calling her.

"Hey," said Britney, "the king's calling you."

Elisha remembered her assumed name. "Oh. What?"

Alex came striding over, pop can in hand, makeshift tie-crown around his head. "What'd I tell you? I said we were going to even things up. Well, it's starting to look that way."

She looked up at him, unable to find anything about him that she liked. "Congratulations."

"Wanna go for a walk?"

"No, thank you."

Britney was shocked. "Sally, I don't believe you!"

Madonna threw in her two bits. "If he was asking me . . . *whoa!*"

"Better listen to 'em," said Alex, reaching out his hand. "Things are changing and I'm worth knowing." He took her by her wrist and tugged her to her feet.

"No, please."

He responded, only half jokingly, "Hey, you don't say no to the king."

With a quick and simple defensive move, Elisha broke his grip on her wrist.

There was a hush. The party stopped. No one moved.

"Whoooa . . . ," came a murmur in the crowd.

Elisha stood her ground, looking Alex in the eye, hoping she had made herself clear.

He leaned forward, raised a hand, about to say something—

"Alex." It was Warren, stepping forward. "Come on. She's Jerry's girl—"

Alex planted one huge hand in Warren's chest and shoved him violently into the guys behind him. "That's *your* opinion. But if you think we have two different viewpoints, then maybe you and me better get together and see if we can come up with a new one."

"Cool," said Ramon.

But Warren was looking past Alex. Everybody was. Alex looked over his shoulder.

It was Elijah, just inside the door. There was no question he'd heard what Alex said. Now everyone was staring at him, and Alex and everyone's eyes said "Trouble."

Alex was in a spot. Everyone was watching him, and he had a throne to defend. He turned to face Elijah directly. "You heard what I said. How about it?"

Elijah looked to his sister for any cues. She was visibly upset and shook her head faintly to warn him.

Elijah stood there a moment, looking at the crowd and then at Alex, and then he couldn't help snickering. "So this is how it works now, huh? You win a fight and suddenly you're dictating opinions and looking for more fights so you can dictate *more* opinions." He said to the crowd, "You see what's happened here? You throw truth out the window and the next thing you know, guys like him start pushing their way in. And if he's the king, what does that make the rest of you?"

Alex started toward him. "I'm gonna shut that mouth of yours."

"Alex!" It was Warren.

Alex looked back. In that window of time, Warren went quickly to Elijah's side.

"I owe you one," he told Elijah.

The sight of them side by side said everything.

Alex had to think about this one.

"Hey, guys, come on," said Madonna, "we're supposed to be having a party."

"What's wrong with a rumble?" said Ramon.

"Alex, you're the king," said Britney. "Don't spoil it. Let's just have fun."

The murmur rippling through the crowd was beginning to lean heavily toward peace and partying.

Brett, his face still puffy, came alongside Alex. "Save it. You're the king. Enjoy it."

> "... if he's the king, what does that make the rest of you?"

Alex listened, his eyes never leaving Elijah and Warren. Finally, relaxing just a little, he said, "Okay." The whole crowd began breathing again. "We've got a party going on here." He shifted his weight forward and pointed in their faces. "But your time's coming, so you be ready."

Elijah persuaded Warren, "You've got a nice face. I've got a nice face. Let's just, you know, leave 'em that way. Come on."

They left.

Alex got back his old smirk and turned to collect the spoils of war.

Elisha was gone. Cher, Britney, and Madonna just shrugged, knowing nothing.

In his room, safe and with his face still nice, Elijah did some figuring, scratching figures on a sheet of paper. "Okay, base of right triangle . . . tangent of the angle . . ." Scratch, scratch, figure, figure. "Archtangent . . . hoo boy . . . no, try it again . . . okay, 47.17. Cool." Then he consulted his time records taken during the day. "Okay, it was high noon here exactly 7.72 hours after it was high noon in Greenwich, England, which means the earth rotated for 7.72 hours. At 15 degrees per hour, that means the earth rotated 115.80 degrees. Greenwich, England, is at 0 degrees longitude, so that puts us at . . . 115 degrees, 50 minutes west of Greenwich. Fabulosity!"

He'd borrowed a road atlas from the library. He flipped it open, hurriedly paged through it, and found the map he was looking for. One quick horizontal measurement, one quick vertical measurement, and he had his answer.

The party was still in full swing in the Rec Center. Hopefully, Elisha would be alone in her room. He turned off the lights, grabbed his flashlight, and went to the window. A few lights were still on in dorm C, but Elisha's window was dark, meaning she was waiting for him to signal.

He blinked out the hailing code: "E E S."

She was watching. She replied, "GLAD YOUR FACE IS STILL NICE."

"RT (Roger That). HAVE LOCATION. PLEASE COPY."

"READY."

"4 7 1 0, 1 1 5 5 0. NORTH CENTRAL IDAHO. ROAD TO WEST. TOWN TEN MILES MAYBE. WORTH A TRY."

"RT. WE MUST GET OUT OF HERE. SUGGEST TOMORROW NIGHT."

"RT."

"LY."

"LY."

Elijah clicked off his flashlight and relaxed on the floor below the window, his back against the wall. "Thank you, Lord."

After all this madness, with so many things denied and unknown, the universe God made was still there, still precise and predictable. Because it was, he knew he and his sister were still on planet Earth, in a real place he could see on a map. Working from that, he also had a pretty good idea of how to get somewhere *else*, and boy, was that comforting.

———

Elisha threw back the covers and hopped into bed, glad and relieved, the numbers Elijah sent her discretely scribbled on her forearm where she couldn't lose them. Before she dozed off, she began formulating ways she could pack and carry food and water. It wasn't unusual for kids to carry extra food out of the cafeteria for late-night snacks, so she and her brother could stock up on provisions during lunch and dinner. Now, if the bears could just be elsewhere. . . .

It would be a long time before she or her brother would sense such peace again, before they would ever rest easy again, or see their rooms, or lie alone in the quiet, in the dark.

———

The next morning, Nate and Sarah stood in the middle of a plowed field at the end of a dirt road in central Illinois. A farmer on his tractor spotted them, which wasn't hard to do—they were the only standing feature in several acres. He steered toward them, they walked, and eventually they met in the wide, open, dusty middle.

"Can I help you folks?" he asked, shutting down the tractor engine.

Nate was carrying some information and a map in his hand. "We understand there used to be an academy around here. The Knight-Moore Academy?"

The farmer started chuckling. "Yeah, there surely was."

"Could you tell us where it is?"

He pointed straight down. "You're standing on it."

That was not good news.

Sarah had to verify, "You mean, right here?"

"The government tore it down two years ago and sold me the land cheap. I'm letting it lie fallow for now. Can't plant it 'til I get all the junk out of it. You shoulda seen the mess they left here. I keep plowing up bricks and concrete and pipes in the ground. Found some wires yesterday. 'Sgood thing I didn't get electrocuted."

Nate dug lightly with his finger and unearthed a piece of charred wood. "Looks like they did some burning."

"They burned the whole thing. Burned it all down, then bull-dozed the foundations, and left a big mess for me to clean up. But like I say, I got it cheap, and it's good ground once you work it."

Sarah looked at Nate. "They burned it."

"Had some complaints about the smoke," said the farmer, "but that's the government. Long as they're the ones doing the polluting, what do they care?"

Nate found a chunk of concrete.

"Yeah," said the farmer. "You find that stuff all over the place." He looked all around as if trying to imagine it. "Hard to believe what used to be here. Buildings, sidewalks, everything. Can I get you folks some coffee or something?"

Nate didn't have to ask Sarah. He could see it in her face. "Thanks. We have to be going. We're, uh, we're in a pretty big hurry."

10

first strike

Elisha slept in late. Breakfast was not vital today; sleep was. Her first class, art appreciation, taught by a male-hating, clipped-haired teacher named Ms. Fitzhugh, didn't start until ten. Elisha felt no need to hurry out of bed. The voices of excited girls in the hall and outside the window kept creeping into her consciousness, but she tried to pretend they were only a faraway part of her dream.

Then Cher shook her awake. "Sally! Sally! Wake up! It's all coming down!"

Elisha opened her eyes, irritated. Cher was prone to overstating things. "What's coming down?"

"Mr. Easley got fired, and we're all going on strike!"

That *had* to be an overstatement. "What are you talking about?"

"Mr. Easley got fired!"

"Who says?"

"Mrs. Meeks! She told us this morning. She said there wasn't going to be any discussion group or volleyball because Mr. Easley got fired, and you know why?"

"No, Cher," Elisha said dully. "I don't."

174

"Because he stole pop out of the pop machine last night! Can you believe that?"

Elisha sat up, brushing her hair aside, trying to make sense of this—as if anything ever made sense in this place. "I thought nobody owned anything so you couldn't steal anything."

"Well, somebody narc'd on him, and he got in trouble, and now he's fired, and Alex has called a strike!"

"What does Mrs. Meeks think about that?"

"She's all for it! She's *joining* the strike!"

Elisha began to wake up and hopped out of bed. "I've got to find my, uh, you know, my friend, uh . . ."

"Jerry."

"Yeah, Jerry."

"I think he's outside waiting for you."

She found Elijah in the field, standing still while girls and boys moved past him, heading for the big iron gate. He was in his uniform, and so was she, but there weren't many uniforms visible this morning. The kids gathering around the gate were wearing anything they jolly well chose to wear; they were making a *point* of it.

"I guess I could loosen my tie," Elijah quipped as they started walking.

"So, are we going to have to take sides on this?"

"Well, maybe we can just *be* there. If we want to know what's happening, it doesn't make sense to be anywhere else."

"That's what I think."

The kids, almost the whole student body of fifty, were gathering, sitting on the grass, sitting against the stone wall, babbling excitedly—and angrily. Mr. Stern and Mrs. Meeks were standing a short distance away, watching everything without getting involved. Alex was striding back and forth, shouting orders, getting people seated, directing traffic. The guy enjoyed being a king, no doubt about that, and the kids responded to him. They also picked up his attitude.

"Hey, look at the suits!" somebody yelled as Elijah and Elisha approached.

Now I'm being stared at because I look nice, Elijah thought. *Oh, well. Warren was in his uniform, and so are some of Warren's friends, so Elisha and I aren't the only ones.*

"We don't know what's going on," Elisha explained.

Alex, tall and mean, in jeans and a tee shirt with the sleeves torn off, was quick to explain. "We're going on strike until they bring Mr. Easley back. No class attendance, no nothing until we get what we want." Then he struck a pose, folding his arms across his chest and eyeing them as he delivered the challenge: "You with us or against us?"

"We wouldn't miss it," Elijah replied.

"Sit over there," Alex told him, pointing to a spot to the left of the gate where half the kids were already seated. Elisha started out with her brother. Alex stopped her. "No, you sit right here."

She exchanged a glance of agreement with her brother and sat on the grass in the front row of the crowd, to the right of the gate.

"And you remember!" Alex warned Elijah. "You and me, it ain't over. I'm watching you!"

Elijah gave him a little salute and found a place to sit.

"Okay, listen up!" said Alex, and the crowd hushed. "Mr. Stern and Mrs. Meeks have something to say."

Alex stepped aside while Stern and Meeks stepped forward.

Stern spoke first. "I've always told you that you are the masters of your own fate. If you do what you have to do and do it right, and don't mess up, I won't stand in your way." He looked at Mrs. Meeks.

"Mr. Easley was a real credit to this school," she said, and got a rousing cheer. "He was visionary. He was kind. He was an example. Unfortunately, there are some on our faculty who don't appreciate his viewpoint on things or his teaching approach, and so . . . Well, I'll be honest. They *informed* on him solely to be rid of him, something I strongly resent."

That got a murmur going through the crowd, a rippling wave of anger and resentment.

"Who narc'd on him?" Ramon demanded, and everyone chorused the question.

"I don't want to get into any names, but I'm sure you all have an idea."

"Booker," came the first voice, followed by others, passing the conclusion along. "Booker." "Booker!" "That creep!" "Surprise, surprise!" "Booker—he's dead meat." "Let's run him out."

"But who told Booker?" somebody asked.

That question poisoned the chatter. The kids started looking at each other suspiciously.

Mrs. Meeks raised a hand of caution. "I ask only one thing. Please—I appeal to your inner goodness, to all that's right and good within your hearts: Please do no harm. Unite, and we'll unite with you. Make your voices heard. But follow a path of peace."

"This is your world, your work," said Stern. "It's not our place to say anything more than that; do what you feel is right, and we wish you the best."

With a look and a step back, they turned it back over to Alex, who led the crowd in applause. "Hey! Stern and Meeks! How 'bout it?"

While the kids cheered and clapped, Meeks and Stern set out across the field toward the office without another word or a look back.

"What do we do now?" somebody asked.

Alex strode back and forth, thinking. "Sit tight."

"How about a list of demands?" Warren suggested.

"Anybody got any paper?" Alex asked.

Maria, the little Hispanic from the volleyball game, passed a pink-bound notepad forward. Alex took it and started his list. "We want Easley back."

"Right." "Yeah." "Right on."

"And I think we should always have free pop," said Brett. That brought a cheer.

"And get rid of Booker!" said Tonya, which brought an immense cheer.

"Yeah," said Alex. "Easley in, Booker out."

"And I want a telephone so I can call my folks!" said Cher. *Elisha* joined the cheer for that one.

Then the chatter began to die down, one voice at a time. Eyes, one pair at a time, began to turn toward the far side of the field.

A tight, short line of adults was coming their way from the campus, walking deliberately, shoulder to shoulder, almost marching.

The crowd went silent, watching, waiting, worrying.

On one end was Ms. Fitzhugh, the art teacher. Not a friendly type. Next to her was Mr. Bateman, the math teacher. He was smart, but kind of fumbly. Mr. Johnson, the facilities man, was stepping right along with them, looking grim. Next to him was Mrs. Wendell, the librarian who also taught yoga. On the other end was Mr. Chisholm, the U.S. history teacher. Very few of the kids had ever seen him, and some had no idea who he was.

Right behind the line of adults, ten big guys, including Rory, Tom, Jamal, and Clay, walked in another line, shoulder to shoulder, looking cool and tough. They were carrying chains in their hands.

And out in front, like a general leading his troops, was Mr. Booker, as grim as ever.

They approached, never breaking formation, until they stood before the kids like a line of riot police. Booker announced loudly, "Mr. Bingham would like to know what this is all about."

And out in front, like a general leading his troops, was Mr. Booker, as grim as ever.

There was a significant silence. Everyone was looking at Alex. Alex was looking at Booker, apparently groping for words.

"Read him the demands," said Brett.

Alex gathered some courage and referred to the little pink notepad. "We have a list of demands! We want Mr. Easley back, we want Booker—" Alex had trouble reading that one, especially with Mr. Booker standing right there. He skipped that part. "We want unlimited pop from the machines, and—"

Booker grabbed the notepad from Alex's hand and slapped his face with it. "You arrogant fool! Mr. Bingham isn't about to grant an audience to a mob of barbarians. Your little demonstration is over as of now!"

The kids in the crowd were eyeing those big guys with the chains and starting to change their attitude. Some were already slinking away, trying to act invisible.

Booker froze them in their tracks. "I did not dismiss you! Return to your places!"

They slinked back.

Alex asked Rory and his bunch, "So what are you going to do now, you traitors? These are your friends. They're your class-mates. You just gonna beat 'em up with those chains? You gonna let this guy push us all around?"

By now, Booker had started laughing—purposely—in Alex's face. "Don't be absurd! These gentlemen are not the barbarians here." He addressed the crowd. "The Knight-Moore Academy, while encouraging freedom and progress of thought, has policies in place to maintain order and discipline. Mr. Easley and his utopian visions are one thing; the will of those in authority is quite another. When I learned of Mr. Easley's indiscretion, I had no choice but to report him. His fate was well deserved."

A wave of anger and disgust swept through the crowd, but of course no one said a word.

"Now it appears we have another indiscretion that must be dealt with, and harshly." He paused long enough to sweep the crowd with his intimidating gaze. "The Rec Center—all the games, all the diversions, all the sports equipment—will be closed and padlocked. The cafeteria, and all the vending machines, will be closed and padlocked. No fun will be available, and no food, for the rest of the day."

That stung everyone. They moaned, they gasped, they exchanged looks of alarm and disbelief.

"Ah. Apparently you forgot where all the fun and food come from. But if you wish, you can show us you remember. I will be in my classroom at three, as always. Any member of the student body who reports to my classroom clean, in uniform, and ready to comply with the academy's policies will be granted amnesty— and perhaps the evening meal. Carefully consider whether it is in your best interests to submit to those in power—" He shot a cutting side-glance at Alex. "—Or to follow the foamings of a would-be emperor with a futile cause. The choice is up to you." He looked over his shoulder at the ten big student bruisers. "Gentlemen. Proceed."

Rory and his gang headed out toward the Rec Center and cafeteria, chains and padlocks in hand.

Booker watched them for a moment, relishing the moment, and then turned to Alex and the crowd. "You're welcome to sit here the rest of the day if you wish. There won't be much else to do. My associates and I will wait until three for your response. Consider yourselves dismissed if you have anywhere to go."

Booker had done it again. For the third time, and with a cruel, silky-smooth style, he had cut away Alex's power and dignity in front of everyone and made him look foolish. One look at the rage in Alex's face, and several kids decided that being elsewhere was a great idea. Warren and his uniformed friends left quickly and quietly, wanting no more trouble from either side. Elijah figured it would be a good time to leave as well. He shot a glance at Elisha, who rose to her feet.

The other teachers and staff began walking away, but Booker was quick to intercept Elijah's path and tell him in a clearly audible voice, "I am sorry to see you in such a situation, Jerry. I did enjoy our talk." He gave Elijah a friendly pat on the shoulder and moved on.

Oh-oh. Hey, wait a minute. Elijah felt a gnawing dread rising in his stomach. He knew which "little talk" Booker was referring to, but he also knew which "little talk" Booker had to be hoping the kids would *think* he was referring to.

The kids thought it, all right. They were all staring at him.

"Jerry . . . ," said Ramon, "you told Booker?"

Elisha piped up, "Of course not! He wasn't even there. He didn't see Mr. Easley open the pop machine."

"He didn't have to," said Alex, instantly regaining his role of bully and head-basher. He planted himself right in Elijah's path. "Everybody knew about it."

"Mr. Booker asked to see me," Elijah began to explain. "It was about something else—"

But Alex had always wanted a good reason to publicly pulverize Elijah, especially since the night before, and now he'd found it. "You've always had it in for Mr. Easley." He gave Elijah a taunting little shove.

"Alex," Elisha demanded, "leave him alone."

Elijah explained, "He was trying to get me to be one of his cops—"

"Every discussion group, you were the one who caused all the trouble," Alex growled. Another shove. "You saw your chance and you took it." A two-handed shove.

Elijah took the shoving and tried to stay cool. "Listen, I know you want a fight, but I'm not—"

OOF! Elijah should have seen it coming: a violent punch to his midsection. He doubled over, pain coursing through every organ in his body. Faintness clouded his vision, his balance left him, and he toppled to the ground, his arms enfolding his stomach.

"Get up!" Alex demanded, about to kick him.

He doubled over, pain coursing through every organ in his body.

Elisha grabbed Alex's arm and yanked him angrily. "You leave him alone!"

He turned and grabbed her right back. "So you want in on this, too?"

Elisha struggled, pulling and kicking.

"Hey," said Ramon, "come on, Alex! Show some class, man!"

"I'll show you something, all right!" Alex grinned.

Elisha brought her heel down on his instep like a thirty-pound spike. That loosened his grip just a little. It was enough. She slipped free. He grabbed for her again.

WHAM! His head cracked against a speeding wall from out of nowhere. "Sally" fell away to the ground as he reeled, staggered, looked around, the earth quaking under his feet. Another blow, this one to his stomach, like being hit with a flying manhole cover. Having gotten Alex's attention, Elijah planted himself between Alex and his sister. "Now, can we please stop this?"

Alex roared like a grizzly and charged, bowling him over like a sapling under a truck tire. They rolled, they punched, they kicked and gouged. Somehow they got on their feet again, fist hitting flesh, arms blocking punches, legs kicking, tripping, blocking. They were surrounded by a circle of screaming, cheering, crying kids—some watching out of sick enjoyment, some watching in alarm, hoping it would end.

Elisha fell back to watch. She'd trained and sparred with Elijah from their preteens, and now she could see where this fight was going—right where Elijah wanted it to go. He was fighting defensively, evading, ducking, blocking, saving his strength, getting in a kick or punch just to keep Alex angry, making Alex put out all the effort, and it was working. Alex was huge and lumbering, with more temper than good sense, and he was getting tired. He was slowing down, getting rubber-legged, losing accuracy in his attack. Elijah kept backing, feinting, ducking, jabbing, leading Alex around inside that circle until the would-be king was ready.

The moment came. Elijah blocked a punch. It was a bad punch, poorly aimed. The big guy wasn't seeing straight. Elijah stayed open, inviting another blow. He could see it coming a year before it arrived, and ducked it. Okay. Time to fell the tree, and none too soon.

Elijah spun and threw a high kick right across Alex's jaw. Alex went down, stunned and exhausted, blood dripping from his mouth. Brett, his second-in-command, knelt down to comfort him and persuade him not to continue.

Around the circle, there was a strange, mixed reaction. Many just stared at their fallen king, at a loss, like fans who'd lost a bet. Some kids, like Ramon, *almost* cheered for Elijah, but now they were suspicious of him, still wondering if he was the snitch. Britney, Madonna, and Cher cheered loudly. They didn't care.

"Don't cheer!" Elijah ordered, his voice hoarse with exhaustion. "Look at us! You think this is anything to cheer about?" He was staggering a little. His nose was bleeding. His burgundy blazer would never be the same. "Just because I win a stupid brawl doesn't make me a better man!" He looked down at Alex, who glared at him through puffy eyes. "No more than you beating me up makes you a king!" He looked at all their faces, hoping to see some shame. "Might doesn't make right, can't you see that? Is this the kind of world you want? War, and stealing, and beating people up? It's stupid! It's not the way to—"

Everyone's attention shifted to the sound of running feet, the sight of adults coming their way: Fitzhugh, Bateman, Johnson, Chisholm, on the run, coming to restore order and looking mad enough to make it hurt.

Ramon took off. Britney, Madonna, and Cher never moved so fast. The circle of kids dissolved like a snowflake in water.

"What's going on here?" Chisholm demanded.

He stopped short, shocked at the sight of Alex on the ground with Brett cradling his head.

"Horrors!" said Ms. Fitzhugh, covering her mouth with both hands as if she would vomit.

Alex was still lucid enough to be sly. He went limp, moaning in pain, holding his stomach.

Brett reported with a dark, feigned sincerity, indicating Elijah, "He tried to take over. Didn't like Alex's leadership, so . . . he attacked him—when he wasn't looking."

Elijah wilted, so disappointed. "Ah, Brett, *come on*."

Elisha was by her brother's side. "That's not the way it was! Jerry was protecting me."

Ms. Fitzhugh nodded her head as if she really understood what had happened, eyeing Elijah with disdain. "Oh. So it's all over a girl! Of course. A young stallion kicking another over his mare."

Alex managed to speak. "I was just talking to her. I don't know what he had to get so upset about."

Elijah sighed. "Does anyone want to know the truth?"

Chisholm stepped forward, grabbing Elijah's arm. "We've seen plenty, young man. Come on."

"Hey!"

"No!" Elisha cried. "What are you doing? You've got it all wrong!"

Now Bateman and Johnson moved in, surrounding Elijah, forcing him along. "This campus has had enough trouble. It's time to clean house."

Elijah, still hoping to find an ounce of reason in any of these people, spoke calmly, "You're making a mistake. If you'll just let me explain my side of it . . ."

Elisha grabbed Mr. Johnson's arm. "Will you listen to me? He's innocent! He was defending himself! He was defending *me!*"

Johnson sneered at that. "Right. It *looks* like it."

Ms. Fitzhugh grabbed Elisha by the arm and held her back. "And you, young lady, are going to your room and staying there."

"What are you doing?" she cried, watching them take Elijah away like a prisoner. "Where are you taking him?"

She heard an ominous clanking of steel, and then, as if by

> "Will you listen to me? He's innocent! He was defending himself! He was defending me!"

itself, like the jaws of a patient, sinister monster, the big iron gate began to swing open.

A searing pang of fear coursed through Elisha like deadly voltage. She knew, she just *knew* that something horrible lay beyond that gate. "NOOO!"

She broke free from Ms. Fitzhugh's grasp and ran after her brother. "No, no, don't take him! He didn't do anything!"

Johnson turned back and blocked her path. He grabbed her, held her. She broke his grip, got around him. He grabbed her by her blazer and held on even as she kicked him, slapped at him, tried to get away.

Ms. Fitzhugh caught up and also took hold of her. "That's quite enough, young lady!"

Bateman and Chisholm took Elijah through the gate and the big iron jaw began to swing shut with a low, electric hum.

With one last twist of judo, one final kick to a shin, Elisha broke away from Fitzhugh and Johnson and ran for what opening remained. "Jerry!"

Through the bars of the swinging gate, Elijah, being hurried along by his two captors, looked over his shoulder and called, "I'll be all right." Then he mouthed the words, "You go! *Go!*" as he nodded toward the unseen road.

The heavy, electronic latch clanged into place the instant Elisha reached it and she fell against the iron bars, gripping them, wishing, praying she could pass through. "Take me! Don't take him, take me!" The bars were cold, cruel, immovable. The gate didn't even rattle when she tugged at it.

The two men were hurrying, nearly dragging Elijah up the long walkway. He looked over his shoulder one last time to give her a reassuring look, to let his eyes say, "I'll be okay," and then, like a curtain closing on the final act, the limbs of overhanging trees closed over the sight of him and he was gone.

As Fitzhugh and Johnson hemmed her in against the bars, she reached through as if she could grab her brother and pull him back, any pretending banished by her anguish. "Elijah!"

They grabbed her, tightly. Weakened by despair and sorrow, she let them take her away.

11

the mansion and
the monster

Elijah couldn't help but be fascinated, looking up at the towering white facade of the mansion as Mr. Bateman and Mr. Chisholm led him down a concrete stairway and through an imposing, oversized basement door. When the metal door clanged shut behind them, a deep rumble rolled up and down the tight, dimly lit hallway like an echo in a mine tunnel. They were deep beneath the mansion now, and Elijah could sense the weight of rock, concrete, and the multistory structure stacked above him.

This was no ordinary hallway. It seemed to Elijah they were in the heart of a huge machine. Thick clusters of electrical wire ran along the ceiling; waterlines, gas lines, air lines, hydraulic lines, and tubing of unknown purpose ran along the base of the walls on both sides. There was a low, electrical hum ringing in the walls. He could hear compressed air moving, water running, fluid surging. "Wow," he said. "What do you guys do down here, anyway?"

They didn't answer, but took him through a doorway into a small bedroom, a slightly nice prison cell. They pushed him down so that he sat on the narrow bed, then let go. "Stay here until we come for you," said Chisholm. He pointed to another doorway at one end of the room. "The bathroom's through there."

"But . . . what's supposed to happen?" Elijah asked. "I mean, do I get to talk to someone, or explain things, or what?"

They didn't answer him. They went out the door, locked it, and left him alone.

All around him—in the walls, in the air, in the floor—was a low, steady, rumbling *life,* much like being aboard a ship or an airliner. *This building isn't just sitting, it's running like a big machine. It is alive.*

If this mansion's a monster, he thought, *then I'm in the stomach.*

Nate and Sarah landed in Coeur d'Alene, in the northern panhandle of Idaho, and parked the airplane in front of Resort Aviation, an aviation service center providing fuel, aircraft rental, scenic tours, and generally anything having to do with aviation or traveling aviators. Inside the office, a young gal with curly blond locks was working behind the counter. Rental rates for Cessnas and Pipers were posted on the wall; navigational charts, airport directories, and tourist brochures were on display. Occasionally, the

This building isn't just sitting, it's running like a big machine. It is alive.

chatter of pilots would squawk from a radio at the far end of the counter, tuned to monitor the airport frequency.

"Hi," said Nate. "We'd like to tie our plane down for a few days."

"Are you the Springfields?" she asked.

That scared them. For secrecy's sake, they hadn't called ahead. How did she know their names?

"Is someone expecting us?" Sarah asked.

"Your ride's here now."

She pointed out the window toward the parking lot. A black car was waiting. The man behind the wheel gave them a subtle wave.

It was Morgan.

They acted pleased to see him to hide the fact that they were alarmed. They hurried out the door and climbed into the car.

"What is it?" Sarah demanded. "What's happened?"

"Easy," said Morgan. "No bad news yet. But it's time for a face-to-face. Go ahead and bring your luggage. I got us some rooms."

The motel was small, one-story, built thirty years ago. The rooms were simple: one bed, two chairs by the window, a small television, a bathroom with a stained sink and a drippy shower.

> **For secrecy's sake, they hadn't called ahead. How did she know their names?**

Sarah took the bed, aching and tired. Nate and Morgan sat by the window after closing the blinds.

"Okay," said Nate, "what've you got?"

"It's a government project," said Morgan. "And then again, it isn't."

Sarah sat up straight. "Morgan! Our children are missing! We've been hopscotching across the country chasing an academy that's never there. We don't need: don't know, might know, can't know! Give us some facts we can work with or let us get some sleep!"

Morgan took her lashing in stride, and pulled out a document. "This might help explain it. It's last year's budget report from the Department of Education."

Nate took a look at it. Sarah flopped back down on the bed and waited to be impressed.

Morgan guided Nate to the third page of columns and figures and pointed to a small, obscure item: *Educational Research Grant*. "Here's a tidy little expense that's been slipping through unquestioned for the past five years. The president was never told about it, and neither was the current secretary of education."

Nate was impressed, and spoke out loud for Sarah's benefit. "Twenty million dollars."

"Per year."

Sarah raised her head. "That's government money?"

"*Our* money," said Morgan. "Your taxes, my taxes."

"Wow!" said Nate, actually happy, tapping the paper. "A fact! A real fact!"

Morgan explained, "Five years ago, the previous president—and several of his cronies in Congress—allotted these funds for research in global education, and part of the program was to set up special laboratories to test their theories with volunteer students."

Now Sarah was sitting up, almost impressed. "The campuses that aren't there anymore."

Morgan nodded. "Exactly. It all looked very legitimate."

Nate asked, "So why aren't the campuses there anymore?"

"Why isn't the Light of Day Youth Shelter there anymore?" Morgan asked rhetorically.

"Why was Alvin Rogers murdered?" Sarah asked.

"Why is the mysterious redhead, Margaret Jones, going by so many different names?"

"And why were our kids taken away without warning, without a trace?" Sarah said with an obvious bitterness.

"Somebody's up to no good and hiding it well," said Nate.

"Even from the president," said Morgan. "Whatever this project was supposed to be, it's turning out to be something else. He and the secretary of education had their suspicions, but with no solid facts, he couldn't order an investigation without looking foolish and drawing vicious attacks from his enemies in Congress, not to mention the media."

"And so the facts are all buried," said Sarah. "Cleared and reforested, plowed under a farmer's field . . ."

"Imploded."

Nate and Sarah looked at him strangely.

"Haven't you heard? The Dartmoor Hotel was imploded just yesterday. It's gone. Demolished."

By now, Nate and Sarah were getting used to such information—almost. They needed a moment to digest that.

Morgan continued, "But if we can find an actual, operating campus and find out what it's really being used for, then maybe we'll get that investigation authorized and stop this monster in its tracks."

"Hmm," Nate mused. "A monster."

"Excuse me?"

"You'll have to read my daughter's English paper."

"Anyway," Morgan continued, "this whole thing *is* a government project in that it's receiving government money, but I would say it's *not* a government project because it's a renegade, carrying out a secret agenda that could be entirely illegal, to put it mildly."

"But we'd have to prove that before anything can be done about it, so we're investigating, but not officially."

"That is where things stand, yes."

"I'm *sort of* impressed," said Sarah.

"Morgan," said Nate, "we're here, but we don't know where to

"Haven't you heard? The Dartmoor Hotel was imploded just yesterday. It's gone. Demolished."

look. Margaret Jones told the kids the academy's up in the mountains, but there are a *lot* of mountains around here."

"Oh, yes! About Margaret Jones! Your information was very helpful. I haven't been able to go through official channels, at least officially, but some friends in the right places have filled in some blanks. She might be in this area."

That did impress Sarah. "I want her, Morgan."

Morgan nodded with understanding. "You'll be the first to know."

"In the meantime . . ." Nate unfolded a U.S. Forestry map of the Idaho panhandle. "We've got a few zillion acres of national forest to comb through. . . ."

———

Elisha, confined to her room, prayed for hope, hoped in God, and did all she could with soap, a washcloth, and a hair dryer to get the grass stains out of her burgundy blazer. Having a vicious brawl on the lawn wasn't good for the Knight-Moore uniform, and she had to please Booker—or at least not make him mad—at the three o'clock meeting.

The door opened, and Cher came in, not at all her usual, bubbly self.

"Oh, Sally! I'm so sorry! I heard about Jerry!"

Elisha was trying to hold herself together, carefully brushing the elbow of her blazer. "We just have to pray they'll let Jerry out and not hurt him—" Her voice broke and she stopped, concentrating on the sleeve of her blazer, trying not to remember the images of Alvin Rogers out of his mind.

"Maybe if Mr. Booker wins."

"Wins?"

"You know, gets his way, and everybody does things by the rules. Maybe then things can be the way they were."

"Cher . . ."

"Mariah."

"Mariah? Can't you just settle on one name?"

"Britney wanted to be Cher, and Madonna wanted to be Britney."

"Why can't you just be yourself?"

"Why can't you?"

Elisha had no answer for that one. "Good question." Back to her original thought, "But . . . Mariah . . . I'm not so sure things can ever be the way they were. They were never any particular *way* in the first place. They weren't supposed to be."

Alice/Marcy/Cher/Mariah sat on her bed, fear in her eyes. "Alex is still mad. He's still talking to Mr. Stern and Mrs. Meeks, trying to get his way, trying to get Mr. Easley back and get rid of Mr. Booker." She sighed, and then admitted, "But I hope Mr. Booker wins. Things might still be weird, but at least I'd feel safe."

Elisha didn't need for Mariah to explain. She felt that way herself. It was a little bizarre, but for all the harshness of Booker's class, there was still a sense of security there, like standing near the edge of a high, precarious cliff, but with a safety railing all around you. You could hate Booker all you wanted, but if you played the game his way, nobody else could threaten you. No one else could mock you or strike you. You could set your books and handbag on the floor and trust they would remain there even when you turned your eyes away. Booker was a tyrant, but his class had boundaries, it had order, and many of the kids could sense that. That was why they hated Booker but still showed up for his class every day, in their uniforms. It was one small island, maybe the last, on this whole campus that felt safe. "So would I."

Mariah jumped up from her bed and started pawing through her dresser drawer. "So one thing's for sure: I'm going to be in uniform!"

Elisha examined her blazer. Not perfect, but it would have to do. Out the window, she could see the roofline of the mansion through the trees. *I won't leave you here, Elijah. God help me, I won't leave you here.*

The low rumble of the monster machine stopped. Just like that. Elijah sat up from a catnap and listened. The stillness was so total it was scary. He checked his watch. He'd been waiting here for two hours.

Well, he thought, *this is a fine mess.* Bateman and Chisholm hadn't come back, and he was beginning to think they never would.

He decided to take a much closer look at this room to learn about it. It was only about ten feet long, maybe eight feet wide.

The ceiling was a little low, maybe six and a half feet. Only one flat, recessed light fixture illuminated the room. The walls were wood paneling, the kind one sees in cheap motels or outdated restaurants—not very attractive, but definitely more homey than concrete. The floor was bare, white linoleum, a little cold to the touch. He looked under the bed. Clean and bare under there. What about the bathroom?

He opened the door and looked inside. It was a little bigger than a phone booth. You had to squeeze around the sink to get to the toilet. The walls were plain white.

He stepped back into the bedroom.

It was blue.

Whoa, hold on, wait a minute.

He blinked and looked again. Blue. The walls, the ceiling, the floor, even the bedspread, were blue. He waited to see if his eyes would adjust to the light. He looked in the bathroom again, then into the bedroom. It was still blue. He went to the other end of the room and looked back toward the bathroom. It still looked blue from this angle.

He repeated his previous action, stepping quickly into the bathroom and back out again, but the room stayed blue. He felt the walls and floor. Blue paint, blue linoleum. The bedspread was blue on both sides. Even the sheets were blue.

He sat on the bed to think a moment. Was he wrong about the wood paneling? Was his memory out of whack?

Just to be sure about everything, he walked over and tried the door. It *used* to be locked, but it wasn't locked now. The hallway outside was wood paneled, just as the bedroom used to be . . . or just as he *thought* the bedroom used to be.

But wait. He didn't remember the hallway having wood paneling. He remembered bare concrete, pipes, wires, tubes, mechanical sounds, an electric hum, dim lighting.

Did he come this way in the first place? Had he gone through a different door?

He looked back in the bedroom again. It was still there, still blue. He opened the door widely, then removed his blazer and placed it at the bottom of the jamb to keep the door from closing all the way. Keeping an eye on the doorway, he stepped slowly and carefully into the hall. Nothing changed.

He ventured down the hall. He did not remember coming this way, or going past these doorways on either side. Were they more bedrooms—or cells—like his? He tried one of the doorknobs. The door opened. The room inside was dark. He felt inside for a light switch, found one, and flipped the light on.

It was a bare little room with a chair and table. On the table was a burgundy blazer. There were grass stains on the elbow and shoulder, and a torn seam down the back. He drew closer, unable, unwilling, to believe it.

The tears, scuffs, and grass stains were unmistakable. His six KMs were still in the inside pocket. He quickly checked the opposite pocket. A crumpled sheet of notebook paper was still there, the paper upon which he'd written the navigational coordinates he'd calculated. He unfolded it, and read his own handwriting:

45 degrees, 6 minutes N

120 degrees, 10 minutes W

They were not the coordinates he remembered. No, no, the latitude was 47 something . . . the longitude was something like 115 . . .

He sat in the chair to think, afraid to move another step.

It's a head trip, he thought. *They're messing with my mind. This is what they did to Alvin Rogers. But how are they doing this?*

Directly in front of him, through the open door, he could see the hallway. It no longer ran to the left and right, but extended straight ahead, as if this room were at the very end of it. It had pink-flowered wallpaper, white wood trim, and a beige carpet.

At a quarter to three, Elisha and Mariah were ready, uniforms cleaned and pressed, hair neatly done, hearts . . . hopeful? Yes and no.

"I just don't want to be afraid anymore," Mariah said as they walked toward Booker's classroom. "I mean, people are good. The kids are good. But they do things that . . . well, that *aren't*

"I just don't want to be afraid anymore," Mariah said . . .

203

good. I don't know why. But I never know what to expect, and I just want to feel safe."

Elisha checked her watch. They had just a few minutes to spare, maybe just enough to say . . . something, anything. She stopped and touched Mariah's shoulder, getting the wide-eyed little blond to look her in the eye. "Mariah, I have to tell you something. If everybody on this campus shows up in a uniform and agrees to follow the rules, then we might be safe for a while. Maybe our rooms will be safe. Maybe I can talk to somebody in charge and get Jerry out of the mansion. But you have to understand, if Mr. Booker and all the other teachers keep teaching there's no right or wrong and all the kids keep believing it, then there's nothing to keep all the trouble from starting up all over again. If there's no right or wrong, then all Mr. Booker has is that yardstick until someone comes along with a bigger yardstick. Do you understand what I'm saying? We're buying some time, maybe, but that's all."

"But people are good. Everybody'll do what's best."

"Is that what you've seen?"

Mariah found no words, but just started walking again.

They hurried down the sidewalk, just as other kids were doing. There were plenty of uniforms around. Britney/Cher and Madonna/Britney were looking sharp, and so were Warren and his friends, but . . .

No. Elisha's heart went sick.

Ramon was wearing a sleeveless tee shirt, jeans, chrome necklace, and an arrogant smile.

Brett was wearing jeans and untucked flannel shirt.

Rory and his gang—Booker's *cops*—were wearing whatever they wanted, and all of them were wearing their ties—as headbands.

"What's happening?" said Mariah, the fear back in her voice.

Elisha couldn't believe what she was seeing. "I don't know." She didn't say it but thought, *Something terrible has happened.*

They went into the classroom. Because all the students were showing up in the room at the same time, the place was getting quite full. All the desks were taken, even Elisha's, and kids were standing around the sides of the room. Elisha and Mariah found a spot against the rear wall and tried to blend. There was an ominous quiet in the room. No joking, no talking, hardly any looking around. Elisha could see fear in many of the faces—fear of speaking, fear of questioning, fear of the next minute.

Rory, Jamal, Tom, Clay, and ten other guys—all of them toughs—were lined up against the back wall, some with arms folded, some with thumbs perched in their pant waists, commanding respect and fear simply by how they looked back at everyone.

Tonya was quite casual, in ragged denim shirt and feeling good about it.

There was an ominous
quiet in the room.

Samuel was wearing a black tee shirt with a heavy-metal rock band image on the front.

Brett's friends from dorm D—including Tom Cruise—were wearing their uniforms, but in any wrong way they could think of. Some had their blazers on backward. Some had blazers above the waist, but jogging shorts below. Marvin, the one Booker had scolded and fined for not having his shoes, was in sandals.

And every one of them was wearing his tie around his head.

Like Alex. He was standing in the back, arms folded, flanked by Rory and his guys, dressed in jeans and a clean, bloodless tee shirt. He still looked battered, but he looked proud. He was waiting.

The room was full now. Full and quiet, like a gang of friends waiting to surprise somebody.

At one minute to three, they heard familiar footsteps approaching. The door opened, and Mr. Booker burst into the room with his usual, regal flair. His gait slowed, however, as he looked about, until he came to a full stop halfway up the center aisle. From the center of the room, with a fist on his hip, he slowly turned, studying the crowd, taking note, meeting any eye that dared to return his gaze. He nodded and raised an occasional approving eyebrow whenever he saw a uniform, but any approval he might have granted was obliterated by the rage and disgust building in his glaring eyes and reddening face. He drew a breath as if he would say something—

Then he saw his privately paid cops all standing with Alex, headbands made from their ties, and he actually flinched, visibly shocked—more shocked and disturbed than Elisha had ever seen him. Seconds passed, and he could say nothing—something else Elisha had never seen. He just stood there staring at Alex, with quick little glances around the room. Elisha knew he was counting uniforms and non-uniforms. She'd already made a quick count herself and knew the news was bad. Booker was receiving that bad news right now, in deadly little doses.

Finally, Alex spoke. "It's over, Booker."

Booker found his tongue, addressing Rory and the cops. "Gentlemen, we had an arrangement."

Rory shrugged and nodded toward Alex. "He's got friends with keys to the cash box. He cut us a better deal."

Stern and Meeks, Elisha thought.

"You can't do this," Booker argued, and his voice sounded weak.

Alex walked forward, flanked by Rory, Tom, Jamal, and Clay, the Big Four. "Can't? You say I *can't?*"

"You . . . you can't!"

"*I* say I *can.* You know how it works, Booker! Come on. Let me hear you say it."

Booker was actually scared! He was backing up the aisle while Alex and his guys kept coming at him. "I'm sure we can reach a consensus here, a fresh viewpoint . . ."

Booker conceded, nodding quickly. "Power. It's, it's all about power."

Alex made a little beckoning gesture right under Booker's chin. "Come on. Say it."

"I don't—"

"SAY IT! What's it all about, Booker?"

Booker conceded, nodding quickly. "Power. It's, it's all about power."

Alex gleefully completed the slogan, tapping his chest. "And now . . . I have it."

They'd reached the front of the room. Booker was hemmed in against his desk. He cried out to the rest of the kids, "Are you going to let this happen?"

Tonya was the first on her feet. "We don't *respect* you anymore!"

The whole room exploded in yells, taunts, jeers. The non-uniforms were all on their feet, shaking their fists in the air, cursing Booker, filling the room with deafening noise. "No Respect! No Respect! No Respect!"

The uniforms were looking about, wide-eyed, hesitant, undecided—it was all so sudden, so brazen, so frightening. Some stood to keep from being different. Some sat, not knowing what else to do.

Alex and his toughs, egged on by the crowd, alive with new energy and madness, grabbed Mr. Booker and dragged him down the aisle toward the door. Alex had Booker's yardstick in his hand, waving it about like a trophy—and like a threat, which excited the crowd even more. As they went outside, the rest of the toughs followed, and then the mob, non-uniforms rushing, uniforms carried along—rushing, crushing, thundering and hollering—out the door like water through a breached dam.

By the time Elisha and Mariah got outside, the mob had surrounded Booker. He was trying to run, tripping, falling, and crawling on the ground, trying to get up, knocked down again, crawling again, covering his head with one arm as Alex and the Big Four kicked, poked, slapped, and shoved him, and as members of the mob got their licks in. Some of Rory's toughs came running from the cafeteria with cases of stolen pop, spreading the cans through the crowd. The kids shook the cans and then popped them open, spraying soft drink all over the deposed teacher, cheering wildly with each blast.

Warren and his friends followed at a distance, stunned, confused, speechless. Other kids in uniforms stayed close to the building as if hoping they could blend unseen into the walls.

The new Britney and Cher, though in their uniforms, jumped right in with the mob, getting in a kick or two and ecstatic when they got cans of pop to shake up.

Mariah was wailing and crying, and Elisha just held on to her to keep her from losing it altogether.

Oh! Here came the other teachers and staff: Fitzhugh, Johnson, Bateman, Chisholm, and even Mrs. Wendell the librarian, running from different directions, shouting, waving their arms, making threats.

"Stop this!" Chisholm yelled, totally indignant. "Stop this at once!"

"Aren't you ashamed of yourselves!" shrieked Ms. Fitzhugh.

"Who's going to clean up this mess?" Johnson demanded.

But the kids were a mob now, beyond words, beyond threats, beyond control. They enveloped the teachers, attacking, slapping, punching, spraying pop then hurling the cans, without reason, without mercy. Chisholm ducked, his arms over his head as pop cans bounced off his body. Ms. Fitzhugh caught a can right in the face, breaking her glasses. Mr. Johnson threw a few punches, but the toughs throwing punches back were bigger than he was.

Then came the turning point, and Elisha saw it happen. She saw it when Chisholm's expression went from outrage to terror; when Booker, tattered, bruised, and soaked with soft drink, bolted and ran for the iron gate; when kids around the field and against the buildings, seemingly on the same cue, began tearing off their burgundy blazers and whipping their ties and scarves around their heads.

The universe had flip-flopped. The adults were not in charge. They were running for their lives, heading across the field toward the big iron gate, Booker in the lead, Chisholm following, Bateman running and helping the limping Ms. Fitzhugh. Mrs. Wendell had kicked off her shoes so she could run—Tonya found one of them and threw it at her. Johnson lagged behind the others, heroically giving the kids a target for their blows and pop cans so the others could escape.

The gate swung open. The adults ran faster than Elisha could even envision an adult running—all out: no dignity, no reserve, no grown-up attitude. They were just plain *running*.

Elisha became very aware of her uniform and Mariah's. She tugged on Mariah's arm. "We'd better get out of here."

As they stole quickly toward their dorm, they could see the gate closing behind the fleeing grownups just in time to save their lives. Alex was leaping in the air, jubilant. The kids were cheering. Others, once wearing blazers, were running to join the celebration.

Mariah was wailing in terror as Elisha pulled her along.

Their world was suddenly different, but *not* better.

12

both/and, either/or

Elijah couldn't find his bedroom cell. Whatever hallway led back to it was gone. He was confused by corners, arches, and doorways he'd never seen before. Every door was unlocked, but not every door went anywhere. Some opened on a blank wall. Another door opened on the same hall he'd left as if he'd never left it. At the end of a hall—while it *was* the end of a hall—he found a door that led to a small indoor courtyard, paved with flagstone, about thirty feet square, with potted plants in the four corners and a three-tiered fountain in the middle of the ceiling. The water was falling up, splashing into a circular, upside-down pond. He reached up—or down—and let the water splatter against his hand. It was wet. It was real.

He was bewildered and amazed. It was an incredible illusion, but a commentary as well. *Both/and*, he thought. A room both right-side up and upside down.

It *had* occurred to him not to move around and see what might happen, but up until now, curiosity had kept him moving and getting more and more lost—as if *lost* were the correct term for it. It was one thing to wander in a fixed, unchanging environment like a forest. It was another to have the environment wander around *him*. But would it continue to wander if he didn't move?

Okay, he thought, *I'll sit still for a while. The fountain is fascinating anyway.*

He found a concrete bench against the wall, tested it first with his hand, and then sat—

I should have known!

He fell through the bench like it wasn't there, tumbled backward and downward like the floor wasn't there, and finally landed—not too hard—on another floor in another room below, flat on his back, looking up at the ceiling that gave no indication he had just fallen through it. The ceiling was covered with red carpet. There was an upside-down doorway with its bottom tight against the ceiling. There was a chair and a potted plant stuck to the ceiling. The ceiling . . . wasn't the ceiling.

Elijah closed his eyes and felt his nerves tingle with instinctive terror as his senses sent him a message: *You're* on *the ceiling, looking down at the* floor. *You're going to fall.*

He argued back, *It's a trick. It's a* trick!

A very good trick, good enough to make him nauseated. His body told him the center of the earth was behind his back; his eyes told him the opposite.

> ## You're on the ceiling, looking down at the floor. You're going to fall.

The door above him opened, and a young man came in, walking upside down on the—well, *his* floor. He was wearing a tattered and stained burgundy blazer, had a bruise on the side of his face and blond hair that really needed a comb. Elijah could just about reach out and touch him.

"Hello?" Elijah called.

The kid looked up—Elijah's down—and all around as if he'd heard a voice, but apparently didn't see anything.

"Hello down there."

The kid looked around again. "Who's there?" He looked up again.

I'm going crazy, Elijah thought.

The kid was Elijah Springfield, *himself*, looking lost and perplexed, wearing the same clothes and looking like he'd just had a terrible fight with someone.

"Can you see me?" Elijah asked.

The other Elijah finally looked his direction and gawked, quite startled. "How did you get up there?"

"How did *you* get up *there*?"

The kid reached up to him. "Are you real?"

Elijah sat up so he could reach down. Their hands touched.

His stomach felt like he'd just done a somersault, and he was standing on the carpeted floor, reaching up toward the ceiling where he'd been.

He was the Elijah he'd been talking to.

His stomach churned and roiled. He was sick and getting sicker. He looked around the room for a place he could throw up and lunged toward the corner in time to give a gift to the potted plant.

Elisha and Mariah, in street clothes again, took a very careful peek out the door of their dorm building. The playfield was empty now. The riot was over, the gate was closed, and things were quiet. A few kids were crossing the campus with snacks in their hands and more pop. Obviously, the toughs who had once locked up the cafeteria still had the keys to open it again.

"What are we going to do?" Mariah asked in a squeaky whisper.

"I want to search the office building for a telephone."

"But everybody said there aren't any phones."

Elisha reminded herself to be patient. "Mariah, since when is the word of anyone on this campus worth anything?"

She thought about that. "You mean they're lying?"

"What a concept, huh? Try to look casual. Here we go."

They walked casually to the library, then casually ducked behind it, then casually moved behind the office building and tried the rear door. It opened, and they found the tool room inside, full of rakes, shovels, a few axes, some hammers, some screwdrivers, sacks of fertilizer, and cans of paint. Another door led them into the main hallway.

They divided up and went from room to room, going through the desks and all the drawers, opening cabinets, moving furniture,

"You mean they're lying?"

217

looking under and behind things, checking for phone jacks, wires, anything. Elisha went through the office where she and her brother had their meeting with Mr. Bingham, the academy dean, and she was surprised at how empty the drawers, shelves, and cabinets were. Mr. Bingham's desk had a few blank yellow pads and two old ballpoint pens in the top drawer, and that was it. Some office. The academy brass hardly used the place.

They searched as far as the front office, but came up empty.

However, the front office had a computer just sitting there idle, with no one around.

"E-mail!" said Elisha.

She took the chair at the keyboard, then reached down under the desk, looking for the on-off switch on the computer tower. She pressed it.

The whole tower scooted backward as if it weighed nothing. She jiggled it, then tipped it, then squatted down, lifted it, and shook it. Except for a loose nut or washer rattling around inside, the tower was an empty box.

She dropped it in disgust, but also curiosity. "It's a dummy. It's a fake."

There were wires going to the mouse, the keyboard, and the wall outlet. There was even a phone jack in the wall, but no line going to it.

Mariah was looking down at her in wonder. "Doesn't it work?"

"No." Elisha was already looking around the room. There was a file cabinet, another desk with some papers and magazines stacked on top, and a copy machine. Elisha clicked on the copy machine. It worked, but it was out of toner and had no paper. She opened the desk drawers. Except for a gardening catalog and a roll of tape, the drawers were empty. The file cabinet was a hollow shell. "Maybe this whole office is a fake." She had to sigh out some disappointment, and then started down the hall. "Come on, let's go."

Mariah followed, a loyal sidekick. "What now?"

"We've got to find a way out of here."

"But there isn't one!"

"There you go again, believing everybody."

They circled around the back of the buildings and reached the far corner of the stone wall, hoping to find any usable route through the woods to whatever road might be back there. There were plenty of unknowns, but that was why they were looking. At this end of the wall, the forest and underbrush were thick, with no obvious trails.

"My, uh, my friend Jerry said he found kind of a trail somewhere."

"I can't go in there!" Mariah whined. "What about the bears?"

Elisha was beginning to feel like a baby-sitter. "Well, just how many bears are there per acre around here? They can't be everywhere at once."

"Everybody who's gone in these woods has seen a bear! They're all over—"

Elisha tapped her gently, shushing her. They listened.

"What is it?" Mariah whispered, afraid of everything by now.

Elisha listened a moment. From somewhere far up the hill

came the *buddluddluddle* of a diesel engine. "It's heavy equipment, like a bulldozer."

"A bulldozer," Mariah repeated, eyes wide with wonder and fear.

Another voice made them jump. "Hello, ladies."

It was Tom and Clay, two of Alex's Big Four, approaching from behind the buildings. Elisha could have kicked herself for not paying more attention and letting them sneak up.

But Warren was with them, gesturing for calm as he said, "It's okay. There doesn't have to be any trouble."

Elisha eyed him carefully. He'd changed out of his uniform, but at least he wasn't wearing a tie around his head. "What do you want?"

There was no malice in his face or his voice. "Alex has called a meeting in the Rec Center and everyone has to be there."

Alex. Elisha was sick to death of Alex. "Well. Alex can toot and light a match for all I care."

Tom and Clay leaned forward menacingly, but Warren intervened, holding them back with a raised hand. "I came along so we could do this politely, without anyone getting hurt." Tom and Clay relaxed—for the moment. "Listen. We *should* be there. Somebody has to talk some sense into this whole thing." He nodded toward Tom and Clay. "And we don't have much choice anyway. *Please* come."

The Rec Center had been reopened with the same keys that locked it. The kids had all gathered and were standing, sitting, kneeling, and leaning all over the lounge area next to the vending machines. Alex, sitting in his favorite spot on the end of a picnic table, was already holding forth as Elisha and Mariah, with their escorts, came into the room.

"We've got to hang together," Alex was saying. "We're the reason this whole academy is here, and if we're one big voice, then those people up in that mansion have to listen to us."

"Well, what about Mr. Stern and Mrs. Meeks?" somebody asked.

"Who?" came a joking response, and a giggle rippled through the crowd.

"Aren't they on our side?"

"They're staying out of it," said Alex. "It's just us now. We are the Voice. We are the Future."

"So who's in charge?" asked Andy, the pool shark.

"Are we gonna vote?" asked Eric, the space game king.

That question brought a wave of hoots and moans. Rory leaned in threateningly and told him, "Hey, don't you have eyes? That's already decided."

Alex continued, "It's time to send a message and tell those people up there what we want."

"What message?" asked Tonya.

"What do we want?" asked Marvin.

Ideas began to float around the crowd amid cheers, and Brett took notes: more fun time, more access to the food, less homework, no homework, volleyball games that could actually be won, no restrictions on which dorms to sleep in.

"And no more uniforms!" That brought widespread agreement, although some of the girls really liked the outfits.

Warren asked, "So what about Mr. Easley? Don't we want him back?"

Alex looked puzzled. "Who?"

Warren repeated the name slowly, insistently. "Mr. Easley. Remember?"

Alex thought for an instant, then shook his head. "Never heard of him." He gazed around the group and let it be known: "Nobody ever heard of him."

An eerie forgetfulness spread from Alex through the rest of his loyal followers—and there were many. "Who?" "Easley?" "Who's that?" "You ever heard of Easley?" "No sir, not me."

"I'm running things now," said Alex. "We don't need any help."

Warren pressed the issue—and his luck. "Wait a minute. You really think Booker and Bingham and all those people up there aren't calling the police right now? You think they aren't going to come back with the police or the sheriff or the riot squad? What makes you think they're going to put up with any of this?"

He was hooted down. "That's *your* truth," said Charlene, and Melinda agreed, "Yeah," and the crowd picked up the chorus.

"That'll be ten KMs, dude!" Alex shouted, and Warren, immediately surrounded by Rory and his guys, produced the coins and backed away into the crowd.

Alex pocketed the KMs proudly, and shouted, "So who's with me?" He got a rousing cheer, but several kids were holding back and he noticed. "Not good enough." His hand went to the neck-tie now bound around his head like a sweatband. "Okay, here's what's gonna happen. You take your tie or your scarf and you wear it like this, or wear it on your arm. You do that, it means you're with us. You don't do it . . . we break your arm."

Kids started fumbling through pockets, fussing and whining, "We don't have our ties!" "I left my scarf in my room!"

"Find something and find it quick," said Alex. "No scarf or tie, no games, no fun, and no food."

"And we break your arm," said Rory.

Handkerchiefs came out. Shoelaces. Several ran back to their rooms to get a tie or scarf. One kid took off his tee shirt and started cutting and tearing it into strips for one KM apiece. The undecideds began deciding, one headband after another.

"Now you're being just like Booker," came a single voice in the crowd.

The silence, the sudden chill, began with Alex as he sat on the table staring across the room. Those near him fell silent as well, and then the kids next to them, and then the kids next to them. In less than a minute, the room was dead quiet and electric with tension.

All eyes were on Elisha, who'd made no effort to tie anything around her head or arm or anywhere else.

"I thought I heard you say something," said Alex.

Elisha looked at all the eyes staring at her and said, "You were the ones making all the fuss about the uniforms, and now you're just making up another uniform."

Alex made only a little wave of his hand, and Brett and two toughs brought Elisha into the center of the room before Alex's picnic table throne. "Where's yours?"

She looked around the room. Britney, Cher, Tonya, Marvin, Eric, Andy, Roberto, Tom Cruise . . . all the kids she'd known these few days, were now wearing something around their heads. Over in a corner, actually trying to hide behind others, Mariah, her sidekick and roommate, was wearing a rag around her head and looking at the floor.

"We're the group," said Alex, "and we've decided everybody should wear something to show unity." Then came the zinger. "You with us?"

Elisha addressed everyone around her, "You should know where this is going to lead, what it's going to turn into."

They groaned and rolled their eyes, murmuring and snickering.

"Okay," said Alex, "what about Jerry? You've got a stake in this: Those people up there have him. You join up with us, we'll put the heat on and get him back."

Cher, who used to be Britney, came forward with a spare scarf, a pretty red one. "Here, Sally. You can wear this. Come on."

Elisha took it, holding it in her hand. There was silence. Waiting.

She could still see Elijah's last look at her over his shoulder. She could remember her promise not to leave him here. She considered what he could be going through, and she almost cried.

"What's it going to be?" Alex prodded.

"Join us," said Cher.

"Come on," said Ramon. "We'll show 'em!"

"Jerry . . ." She felt like a liar and a coward not using his real name. "Jerry would have to bow to you. He'd have to say you're right, and he won't do that. And neither will I." She handed the scarf back to Cher. "Thank you."

All eyes were on Alex. Brett asked him, "So what are you going to do?"

Alex was looking through the crowd at Warren, who stood silently, out of the way, but still wore no headband. "Give her something to think about."

It took four tough guys to drag Warren out of the building and hold him while Rory and Clay brought cans of paint from the tool room. With wild yells and whoops, they threw him on the grass and doused him with the paint, throwing in some brutal kicks while they were at it. Alex made sure everyone remained in front of the Rec Center and watched, especially Elisha.

"*Unity*," he said. "That means we find the traitors, and we deal with 'em. And . . ." He wrinkled his brow as if trying to remember something. "Who was that guy she was talking about? Anybody ever heard of Jerry?"

All the kids looked blankly at each other, asking each other. No one had a clue.

"Right. Feels true to me." He handed Elisha a push broom and told her loud enough for all to hear, "Keep the floors clean, and the toilets, too, and maybe we'll give you a break." Then he told her quietly and up close, "And I'm doing you a real favor. Better remember that."

Elijah was outdoors, or at least, he thought he was. There was a sky above him—sometimes. There was soft earth below him—sometimes. The temperature was strangely warm, the smells all wrong, the sounds—it was so noisy out here! He heard wind in the treetops, but didn't feel it. He was in the middle of a forest, but couldn't touch it. When he walked forward, he went backward. He couldn't close his eyes for very long because the dark hurt them.

He didn't know how he'd gotten here, whether through a door, or a curtain, or around a corner, or perhaps by waking from a dream only to enter another one. Looking in all directions, he saw only the forest, but no doorways, no portals of any kind. Left and right, north and south, rotated around him, first one direction, then the other. Shadows shifted as if the sun were rambling aimlessly around the sky.

The earth had been level enough to stand on, but suddenly, with only his feet to tell him, the level ground became a hill. He lost his balance and fell against a tree, but the tree didn't stop his fall. He rolled on the ground as if down a hill, until the ground or gravity or his tumbling senses changed again and he rolled back *up* the hill, unable to stop himself.

The wind was rushing high above. Rushing. Rushing. Rushing.

Bruised, dizzy, nauseated, he went limp, trying not to move, not to add any effort or energy to this tumbling universe around him. His body kept moving anyway, rolling, then crawling, then walking, forced to find earth beneath it or a handhold above, or even the next breath of air.

The wind kept rushing, rushing, rushing.

He clamped his eyes shut. The glare of the darkness hurt them, but he held them shut and tried to think, tried to find any sensible thought, real sensation, or unjumbled memory. Every nerve, every sense told him the earth had become a raging sea around him. He tried to shut it all out, tried to dig for a word, a thought, a memory.

The Lord is my Shepherd, he thought, amazed that the words were still intact somewhere in his spinning, crazed head. *I shall not want.*

He tried to speak the words out loud, but the wind carried them away before he could hear them.

The wind rushing, rushing, rushing.

He was falling again. He opened his eyes and saw tree branches whipping toward him. They slapped him, scratched him, lashed him. He tumbled, spun, crashing through them. He grabbed a limb; it tore loose from his hand. His body smacked into another, slowing his fall enough to grab on. His feet flew past him, and he was dangling in space—the sky below him, the ground above—feeling a new terror: There is no stopping when you fall into the sky.

He was falling again.

The Rec Center was in full swing, the lights flashing, the music pounding, the games gobbling KMs.

Elisha kept the broom moving, constantly dodging the running, ambling, dancing, kicking feet, gathering up candy wrappers and pop cans that fell out of the dark like snowflakes. A few cans were tossed directly at her; some of the feet purposely kicked cans away from her broom so she had to go after them. Sprayed pop and spittle were soaking through her shirt. She kept moving, kept working, kept ducking danger—

Everything stopped. The music growled down to silence, the video games went black, the lights went out, the girls screamed.

The power was out. The room was in total darkness.

Pandemonium. Hands groping, people yelling, girls screaming. From somewhere in all the noise and confusion, Alex was shouting, "Quiet, everybody! Quiet! It's okay!" He started calling for his crew, getting them to work on the problem.

In a moment, everybody might quiet down and get reoriented. They might come up with a plan for dealing with the power outage.

Right now, nobody knew what to do about anything and couldn't see six inches.

Girl, it's now or never.

Elisha remembered an exit only ten feet to her right. She dropped her broom and moved right, bumping one body in the dark, but making it to the wall. With just a few seconds of searching by touch, she found the door and slipped through it. She wasn't the only one.

It was after dark, but with the stars and moon, not nearly as dark as inside the Rec Center. The power was out everywhere, the whole campus dark, but she was still in the open and visible, not safe. She ran toward the library, and could see two, maybe three other kids running at panic speed across the field. Rounding the corner of the library, she spotted a girl trying a door, whimpering when she couldn't open it, racing to another door, yanking it open, and ducking inside. Elisha almost ran into another girl—one of Warren's friends—running down the alley between the library and dorm D. The girl didn't even look at her, didn't even slow down, but ran straight into the woods, pushing, thrashing, disappearing into the undergrowth. Behind the dorms, the lid of a trash bin clanged shut right before a boy—it might have been Tom Cruise—knocked, whispered, and got some help climbing in from whoever had climbed in before him.

Elisha kept running. She had one quick stop to make in her dorm room and then—

She heard a scream from the woods and the growl of a huge animal, and that sound seemed to stir up more. From the thickly wooded hills all around the campus came the eerie, haunting echoes of animals in the night: the low growls of bears, the blood-chilling screech of cougars, the howls of wolves. The mountains had come alive, and the sounds seemed so close.

She stole into dorm C and down the dark hallway, barely able to see the doors, counting them until she came to room 4. She made it inside, found the flashlight, this time on Mariah's bed, and dropped to the floor, shining the light and reaching up under her bed.

Her radio was still where she'd hidden it, tucked among the bedsprings. She pulled it out, groped for the switch—

She dropped it—

It fell no more than a foot, hit the floor, and broke open. Metal washers scattered outward like mush from a dropped pumpkin. She grabbed the fallen radio case, and it was light, empty, just a thin half-shell of plastic.

Her hands trembled. She couldn't fathom what she was seeing, couldn't bring herself to believe what it meant.

Her radio had been gutted. Except for one battery still wired in to make the little red light come on—to fool her and Elijah into thinking the radio still worked—there was nothing inside the radio but metal washers and modeling clay.

With the shock wrenching her insides, she fell back against the wall, sick and shaking, holding the remnants of the only contact she might have had with the outside world. Slowly, wretchedly, she began to realize that every time she thought she was sending a message, she'd only been talking to a dead little box crammed with clay and washers.

Worse yet, *they knew*. Whenever, however those people in that big mansion did this, they had to know that she and her brother were not ordinary runaways. She and Elijah were never a secret to them. They knew all along.

Her head sank, her hands went limp, the empty radio case clattered to the floor as a different kind of darkness invaded her, numbing her mind, constricting her soul. She'd been in danger before and knew what fear was. She'd been on her own before and knew what it was like to be alone, at least for a while. But fear and loneliness were nothing compared to this.

Despair was trying to take her. Despair. Could anything be worse? Could there be any pit so deep, any trap so inescapable? As long as she had hope, she could handle fear and loneliness. But despair went straight for her hope, stealing it from her, leaving her with nothing but a blackened room, enemies all around, predators in the woods, nowhere to go, and no one to hear her cries for help except . . .

"Oh Jesus," she prayed, and by now she couldn't help but weep, "what am I going to do? *What am I going to do?* Help me. *Please* help me."

A miracle would have been so welcome, perhaps an angel to suddenly barge into the middle of this madness, offer some explanation that would make sense of it all, and carry her and her brother out of this nightmare and to safety, to Mom and Dad, to the ranch and home.

But there was no angel, no miracle.

She just had to cry, so she let go, abandoning herself to her sobbing, her hand over her mouth lest the sound of her anguish carry outside the room.

"I found a phone."

"Sally," came a voice.

She held back a sob. *Dear Jesus, no. Don't let them find me.*

The voice came nearer. "Sally. Are you in here?"

It was Mariah. Friend or foe? What should she do? *Lord Jesus*—

Too late. Mariah came into the room, stumbled over her, and then plopped down beside her on the floor, her back against the bed. Then *she* started crying. "It's all such a mess."

Elisha wiped her own tears and pulled in her sobs. "What is it, Mariah? What's gone wrong—I mean, besides everything?"

"The big people up in the mansion have turned off all the electricity. They're trying to starve us out or freeze us out or something."

"Mariah . . ."

"Joan."

Elisha was about to get mad. "Do we have to play that stupid game now?"

"I'm not playing a game! That's my name!" She whimpered and sniffed as she said it, "I'm Joan Matheson. I live in Port Orchard, Washington, and I'm fifteen, and I ran away from home two weeks ago and I'm scared."

Elisha wasn't sure this was happening. Was she actually hearing someone telling the truth? "Joan, are you being honest with me?"

"Yeah."

"Then you do know about Jerry?"

"He's your boyfriend and now he's up in the mansion."

"And what about Mr. Easley?"

"He used to work here but he got fired."

"And what about the kid who was taken up to the mansion before Jerry and I got here? Did that really happen?"

"Yeah."

"What was his name?"

"He wanted us to call him Mick, but Alex called him Alvin."

"Tell me about Alex. Is that his real name?"

"No. It's Harold."

"Joan . . ." Elisha's voice cracked. Her tears returned. "My name isn't Sally. It's Elisha. Elisha Springfield. I'm from Montana, and I'm scared, too."

"Some of the kids are hiding. Alex—well, Harold, but now he wants everybody to call him Alexander—he says we'll be all right if we do what he tells us, but . . . who says so? You saw what he did to Warren. He could do that to anybody—anybody he doesn't like, or anybody who says something, or maybe . . . what about the girls? What if Alex or Rory or some of those guys want to do something to one of us? Who's gonna stop 'em?"

Elisha hadn't noticed yet, but the despair had left her. "We have to keep that from happening."

"How?"

"We have to do whatever it takes. We have to think, and look, and pray, and let God show us what to do."

"I found a phone."

Elisha's next word stuck in her throat. It took a conscious decision to exhale and then bring in fresh air. "What did you say?"

233

They hurried through the back door of the office building, past the tools, shovels, rakes, hammers.

"I found it in the closet," Joan whispered. "I was going to hide in there, but then I thought I should find you and tell you."

They hurried into the front office, their one flashlight guiding their way, and there it was, resting on the computer desk where Joan had left it.

Elisha grabbed up the receiver and put it to her ear. The line was dead. "It isn't working."

Joan was nervously looking around the room and said nothing.

Elisha traced the telephone's cord. "Well. It isn't even plugged in."

"Oh, yeah. I didn't think of that."

"Wait! Wait a minute!"

Elisha ducked under the desk, shining the beam of her flashlight up and down the wall until she found what she'd seen there earlier: a phone jack. She plugged the phone line in, backed out from under the desk, and grabbed up the receiver.

A dial tone.

Elisha wanted to cry again, but that wouldn't help right now. She tapped out a number—her dad's cell phone—and waited. The line started ringing.

Joan was nervous, drumming her fingers on the counter, looking down the hallway.

Ring . . . ringgg . . .

From the hall, a flashlight beam clicked on and began playing about the room. The beam caught Joan's face, her frightened eyes wide in the light.

"She's here," Joan said.

Elisha heard a connection. "Hi, this is Nate Springfield," came her dad's recorded voice. "I'm sorry I can't come to the phone right now . . ."

The beam of light came into the room and hit Elisha in the eyes, blinding her. She raised her own light and shined it back.

In quick flashes, in quaking light, like a ghostly, floating image hovering behind that tormenting beam, Alex's leering eyes looked back at her.

". . . but if you'll leave a message, I'll get back to you . . ."

Another light clicked on behind Alex. She couldn't see the face, but it was somebody big.

A third light clicked on near the front door. "Too cool." The voice was Rory's.

She searched with her light and found Alex's face once again. He was looking at Joan. "Good job."

No. What was happening?

"Now you better get out of here," said Alex, and Rory opened the front door.

Joan hurried to leave. Elisha caught her face one last time in the beam of her light. Joan looked back, shaking her head feebly, her face a tangle of confusion. "I was afraid."

She ran out the door, and Rory closed it.

In the telephone, Nate's voice mail beeped for the message.

"You guys hold her," said Alex.

13

something true,
someone blue

Dad—" Elisha said, but Rory and the big shadow behind the flashlight were closing in on her.

"That phone doesn't work!" Alex laughed.

The big shadow got to her first and grabbed her with one huge hand. Thankfully, the other hand was still holding a flashlight, so Elisha could move a little.

She moved her knee in a lightning fast upkick, aiming for the center of this guy's existence. By the way he hollered and let go of her, she knew she'd connected. A blow to his throat with her flashlight sent him reeling backward.

But Rory was right behind him. She leaped sideways, putting the desk between them. He missed his first grab, and she nailed the back of his head with the telephone receiver. She shined her flashlight on her left forearm. The numbers Elijah had given her were still there, written in blue ink in a safe place she wouldn't lose.

Rory was coming around again. She could see his face in the bounced and reflected light now flying about the room. She whipped the phone receiver across his jaw and then kicked him in the chest. He stumbled backward.

"Four seven!" she yelled into the phone.

Alex grabbed her from behind, his big arm around her neck. She cried out, then automatically whipped her leg behind his and tripped him backward. They both went down, but when his back caught the corner of the empty filing cabinet he weakened enough for her to wriggle loose and bang his forehead with the butt of her flashlight.

"One zero, one one—" she said, struggling to her feet in the dark.

She leaped on top of the desk, taking the high ground, and from there, kicked Rory in the face. He staggered away, holding his nose and cursing. "Five five zero! And I love you!"

Alex was coming at her from behind. The big shadow was back, coming at her from in front—she could see his silhouette against the window.

She emptied her hands, ran along the desk, bounded off the copy machine, and dove right into the shadow's chest. He fell backward through the window, crashing the glass. She hung on to his shirt for all she was worth, tucked her head in, and rode him through, letting him take the beating and the cutting and the impact of the sidewalk outside the window as the shards of glass followed them, tinkling on the concrete.

He wouldn't be getting up soon. She somersaulted onto the grass, got to her feet, and took off across the field.

> "One zero, one one—" she said, struggling to her feet in the dark.

There was no question, no option, no choice, no doubt: She was going to reach the mansion, she was going to find her brother, they were going to get out of this place or die in the process.

———

Elijah had fallen into the sky, but now mud, sand, and weeds surrounded him; thorns jabbed him like stinging nettles. He got to his feet, trying to escape the pain.

His mind told him, *insisted*, that he was running, deliberately putting one foot in front of the other, even though the ground did not move under his feet, or turned when he did not, or inclined steeply upward though he saw no slope before him. Even when he closed his eyes, he could see. He yelled, cried out verses of Scripture, but he heard nothing. The pathway became a precipice and he tumbled headlong, falling through space. He was under water. He tried to swim; suddenly his groping arms were pulling him forward through hot, dry sand. The sky above was red like a sunset, the earth below an eye-buzzing purple—then green, then gray, then red as the sky turned green.

Where he was, or why, or when, or how, he could not know. There were no days, no hours, no moments, no way of knowing, no chance for knowing how long he'd been here.

Been where?

No place, at no particular time.

I am Elijah Springfield. His mouth formed the words, but the wind carried them away. He once knew of a sister, a father and mother, a ranch where something, anything, could be known for sure.

But those people, and that time, and that life were becoming . . . nothing. Non-things. A vacuum, like space.

He groped desperately about in his mind for knowledge, something he could know, something true. But there was no knowledge, no thought, no reason. There was nothing here but terror, endlessly repeating cycles of it, layer upon layer of it, with more, more, more to come, in swirling, kaleidoscoping sounds, images, and sensations, pulsing, pounding, surging, throbbing like a swollen thumb.

The only reality.

Elisha ran to the corner of the wall where the wall met the forest—thick forest, with huge trees, prickly branches, clinging underbrush, and enclosing darkness. Penetrating that nether world seemed impossible, but her brother had been here. He'd been up this hill, he'd encountered a bear. There had to be a way.

She pressed into the brush, groping with her hands, pushing against limbs and branches with her body, pressing on with nothing to lose. The mansion was built by people and lived in by people, and people needed roads, phone lines, transportation. Somewhere beyond these trees there had to be a real world. Elijah might have seen it, and she was going to find it.

She could see the lights from the mansion off her left shoulder, but still no gap in that stubborn stone wall. She kept climbing the hill, breaking and snapping through dry branches, stumbling on loose rocks, groping as if blind, guarding her face and eyes with her forearm.

Then, up ahead, she could see the branches of trees in the amber glow from one of the mansion's yard lights, as if a clearing—such as a road—was allowing light from the mansion to penetrate the forest. All right! It might be the road her brother almost reached before—

Oh, no. What was that?

Closer than she could believe, she heard a low, close-to-the-ground snuffing, then a snorting. Some bushes rustled. Some twigs snapped.

Oh, great. Remember, girl, what do you do, what do you do? Uh, yell, make some noise, scare it away.

Elijah said it didn't work.

The critter growled. She could hear the bushes rustling closer, the pounding of its big feet on the ground.

She couldn't see where it was, but she could hear it, enough to run in the opposite direction, crashing through limbs and brush, stumbling over fallen logs and rocks. A log tripped her; she went down, got to her feet, ran. All dark ahead of her, she couldn't see—

Oof! She found the wall in the dark, her outstretched arms taking the impact. That thing was still out there, huffing and snorting, looking for her. She groped along the wall, trying to find any way that she could climb it.

AWW! She dropped, as through a trapdoor, quicker than she

could realize what was happening, slipping, sliding, dropping down a bizarre rabbit hole, her eyes useless in the total dark. She was just beginning to think this felt like a waterslide without the water when—

Bump!—she landed on a smooth floor, tumbling, sliding, squeaking to a stop.

It was quiet, and totally dark. She'd escaped the bear, but where was she? It sounded like a room; she could hear the echoes of the walls in the air. But also, she could discern a steady, mechanical hum as if she were inside the belly of a huge machine.

———

The party in the Rec Center was over. Some kids had managed to return with flashlights, but the games were all dead. There was no more music. Besides the fear and anxiety, boredom was setting in.

"Where's Alexander?" Ramon asked.

"He went to take care of some business," Brett answered, trying to hold things together in the boss's absence.

"Well, he'd better get some business done here or we're all—" He clammed up when two big guys leaned into his space. "Hey, cool it, guys, I'm just talking."

"Well, stop talking," said one.

Two flashlights came through the door, carried by two muggers who looked like they were the ones who'd been mugged. Alexander was limping with a sore back, and Rory was holding a cloth to his bleeding mouth.

243

Brett started to ask, "How'd it—Never mind."

"She ran toward the mansion," said Alexander. "Thinks she can get away . . ."

"Where's Clay?"

"We carried him to his room. He'll be okay. He fell through the window."

Ramon was only the first to start asking questions. "So what do we do now?"

Kids were coming out of the dark, gathering like moths around a lamp. They were bored, scared, disillusioned, hungry, and restless. "When do we get the lights back on?" "They're after us, aren't they?" "We're all in trouble now." "How are we going to cook anything?" "There's no hot water." "What are you going to do, Alexander?"

"They're just trying to scare us!" Alexander answered. "They're trying to break us down, make us give up." He yelled so they could all hear, "But we're not going to give up! We've won the first round, and tomorrow morning we're going to win the second!"

Brett asked for all of them, "What's the second?"

Alexander could see lights on up on the hill. "They think as

> **Kids were coming out of the dark,
> gathering like moths around a lamp.**

long as they can hide behind that wall they can play around with us and put us off. Down here, we're just their puppets. But up there, up in that mansion, that's where the strings are. That's where the power is." They all looked at him, caught up in his spell, awed by his visions. "Come on. I know what to do."

———

Nate and Sarah were driving through Coeur d'Alene, returning from a tedious visit to the local branch of the U.S. Forest Service, their last stop of the day. They'd spent the day going over maps, making phone calls, grappling with bureaucrats and checking any discrete sources that would come to mind, but no one anywhere—not the forest service, or the sheriff's office, or the power or phone companies, or the local gas station attendants or restaurateurs—had ever heard or seen anything about a summer academy for high school kids or runaways. Now it was late at night, they were tired, and beyond frustrated.

"Let's call Morgan," said Nate. "It may be more fruitful to help him track down Margaret Jones."

Sarah picked up his cell phone. "Oh-oh. We missed a call."

She pressed the button to play back the message, listened, and her face went pale. "PULL OVER!"

———

On the west edge of Coeur d'Alene, Mr. Morgan stepped out of his big black car and looked toward the car parked just ahead of his. The driver, head down to hide his face, pointed toward the classic old house across the street and then drove away.

"Thank you, sir," said Morgan, watching the car shrink in the distance.

He opened the passenger door of his car, and a matronly woman got out. Together, they walked across the street and up the steps onto the broad front porch. Some lights were still on. Apparently the occupant was enjoying a late TV show and not expecting callers. That was fortunate.

Morgan rang the doorbell.

The sound of the television cut off. A moment later, the door opened a crack and a redheaded woman looked out.

"Very sorry, ma'am, please pardon the intrusion," said Morgan.

"And who are you?" she asked, wary and bothered.

"My name is Morgan." He showed her some ID. "This is Emily Perkins, a forensic consultant assisting me." He then referred to some papers in his hand: color copies of Knight-Moore brochures and a photograph of Kathy Simons holding a

> "My name is Morgan." He showed her some ID. "This is Emily Perkins, a forensic consultant assisting me."

trout. "Kathy Simons? Or should I address you as Suzanne Dorning? Or perhaps Margaret Jones?"

She looked at his evidence and said nothing, but her face said everything.

"I work with a team of private investigators, and since our investigation thus far seems to be leading to you, I thought it might be in your interest to make sure our information is correct. May we have a chat?"

She sighed and let them in.

Nate and Sarah were forcing themselves to remain calm, to think, to work with the information they'd just received from Elisha's frantic, tortuous phone call. They could hear the struggle, the cursings and yellings in the background, the sounds of kicking, tripping, crashing, falling, the sound of the receiver being dropped, followed by a horrible crashing of glass. It sounded like the end of their daughter, and now, all they had was a hodge-podge of numbers staring at them from Sarah's notepad.

Nate listened to the error message from his cell phone. "It's not a phone number, not even international. Did we miss any of the numbers?"

Sarah shook her head. "It's all she gave us. She finished her message. She said she loved us at the end, right before we heard the crash. It has to be enough."

They stared at the numbers.

"Forty-seven," Nate mused.

"Four hundred, seventy-one . . ." Sarah tried. "Four thousand, seven hundred and ten."

"Forty-seven and ten." He froze. He tapped on the numbers with his pen. "That's it. THAT'S IT!"

Sarah was already catching on. "Forty-seven and ten . . ."

Nate grabbed his pen and divided the digits into groups. "Forty-seven and ten. One hundred fifteen and fifty."

"Latitude and longitude!"

Nate was already scrambling for the forest service map. "47 degrees, 10 minutes north latitude, 115 degrees, 50 minutes west longitude! Oh, kids, I love ya! I love ya!"

He located the coordinates on the map. "Closest town is Stony Bend, a good distance southeast of here. Call Morgan, tell him where we're going."

He tossed Sarah the map and hit the gas pedal.

———

Minutes passed, enough for Elisha to conclude nothing further was going to happen unless she made it happen. With the floor the only thing known, she lay belly-down and began inching along, reaching out in front and to the sides, probing and exploring.

BANG! A loud noise and a sudden flood of light nearly scared her to death. A wall panel had opened, vanishing into the ceiling in the blink of an eye. Squinting in the light, Elisha could see she was in a small, square room. At one end was the bottom of the slide that brought her here; at the other end, with the panel raised, was a long, narrow hallway, washed with an amber glow from hundreds of tiny ceiling lights.

Squinting, trying to get accustomed to the light, she could vaguely see someone walking up that hallway, coming toward her. It was a man. No, it was a young man. He was wearing a burgundy blazer. He kind of walked like her brother.

It *was* her brother!

She got to her feet, wanting to run to him, but she was wary of walls that could disappear, lights that could blind, trapdoors that could open. She just wasn't sure about this place. "Elijah? Elijah, are you all right?"

He put a finger to his lips. "Sh. Come on." He beckoned to her.

She ventured into the hall. It looked solid enough. She could touch the walls. The floor was solid beneath her. She quickened her pace. Elijah was smiling at her, encouraging her. He looked pretty tired, but okay.

"Where are we?" she asked in a hushed voice.

"Come on," he answered.

"Where are we?"
she asked in a hushed voice.

He turned and disappeared into a side passage. She hurried to catch up, rounded the corner, and saw him go through a door. She broke into a run, got to the door, and hurried through—

BANG! The door slammed shut behind her—a short little scream escaped her throat—and she was blind again, in total darkness, feeling like she'd walked right into a trap . . . but . . . how could her brother . . . ? "Elijah! Talk to me. What's going on?"

A voice from somewhere said, "Okay, here she is."

"Hello?" she called.

"Hang on, Elisha," said the voice. She didn't recognize it. "Just stand there a minute."

She heard the rumble of another wall moving on rollers. A vertical slit of dim, rose-colored light appeared, then widened, expanding from right to left like a curtain drawing back. She saw red, blinking lights far away in the dark, then red digital readouts, huge cabinets and equipment racks, more glowing lights, TV monitors, patch cables, knobs, switches. The wall kept moving, the vision broadened before her, and she was awestruck; stretching into the semidarkness were two rows of control consoles with a dozen technicians wearing headsets, sitting at computer screens, TV monitors, and daunting control boards with thousands of knobs, dials, faders, toggles, readouts. On the far wall, huge video screens were flickering from one view of the academy campus to another.

I'm either in a really big TV studio or a spaceship, she thought.

A man dressed in black approached her. He was thin, a brainy sort, with his hair tied in a long ponytail down his back. "Hello. Let me show you to a chair."

He guided her to a corner of the room, to a comfortable stuffed chair on a small platform, surrounded by a curved, green wall, and pleasantly lit. It looked like a small set for a TV talk show, but with only one chair. She looked the chair over carefully, then sat in it.

"Comfortable?" he asked her.

"Yes," she answered, still too blown away to say anything else. Then her first question finally came to her. "What happened to my brother?"

Another voice from amid all that blinking, glowing equipment answered, "Your brother is here with us."

That voice she recognized, and now she could see his face bathed in orange light, the blinking lights and red digital readouts reflected in his reading glasses. "Mr. Bingham."

"Welcome, Miss Elisha Springfield. Please make yourself comfortable."

His wasn't the only familiar face. Just behind him, looking very pleased, even victorious, was Mr. Booker, none the worse for wear, his formal, imposing air gone, his hair combed differently, like . . . like an actor out of costume. Next to him, perfectly comfortable in Booker's presence and apparently still employed, was Mr. Easley, now in long pants and shirt, no longer the "phys-ed" guy. Mrs. Meeks—or whoever she really was—was occupied at a control station, wearing a headset, minus her bookwormish glasses and hair-in-a-bun. Mr. Stern, wearing a headset and carrying a clipboard, came and stood with Booker, Easley, and Bingham, smilingly sharing the sight of a ragged, scratched-up, nearly exhausted girl in old jeans and an army-surplus khaki jacket.

"We'll get to you in a moment," said Bingham. "I'm sure you're wondering—"

"They're in the tool room," reported a technician, tweaking dials and looking up at the big video screens.

Elisha watched in amazement. The four big screens provided multiple, wide-angle views of the tool room, and she could see Alexander, Brett, Ramon, and Rory gathering up the rakes, shovels, axes, hammers, and anything else they could lay their hands on, passing them outside to the other toughs.

"Yes," said Bingham, addressing Booker, "thanks to your little recruitment meetings, they all know about that tool room." He looked at the large, digital clock on the wall. "Nearly three in the morning. They might pause to get some sleep, but in any event, I predict they'll approach us at first light."

Booker chuckled as he shook his head. "So predictable."

Booker chuckled as he shook his head. "So predictable."

Bingham wasn't one to smile, but he did appear pleased. "Be glad. A different selection of kids might have killed you."

Booker laughed. "Oh, I *was* scared for a moment."

"We all were!" said Ms. Fitzhugh, entering with a fresh cup of tea.

There was laughter—from a small audience. Elisha looked to her right, and along the back wall, facing the big screens, was a sizable group of faceless people sitting in the dark.

Bingham spoke to them, apparently in the middle of a lecture. "We interviewed and handpicked every child. This year we were looking for a particular, modern personality, the media-oriented, amusement-dependent, consumer type; a child who hears with his eyes, thinks with his feelings, and has been made to believe there are no absolutes, and therefore no right or wrong. Children from dysfunctional families were preferred; runaways provided an ideal subject pool." He looked toward the big screens as a technician cued a recording.

Elisha's mouth dropped open. There, while one big screen continued to show the raiding of the tool room, another big screen replayed footage of the red-headed woman, Margaret Jones, talking with Ramon, then Britney, then Alice/Marcy/Cher/ Mariah/Joan, then Harold "Alex" Carlson and Alvin Rogers over a bowl of soup in a youth shelter, asking them questions about right and wrong and showing them a brochure.

"Using what we've learned in the previous years, we've been able to isolate and encourage a personality type that doesn't think but only follows, and believes any lie as long as there is pleasure attached to it."

On the screen, Alexander was sitting on the picnic table, announcing the headband requirement. Kids all around him grabbed, ripped, or cut anything they could find to wrap around their heads.

"Oh, and please note this result."

Elisha saw herself and some others in a muddy, dark picture, their faces blinking in and out of the dark as unsteady flashlight beams flashed around the room. The camera zoomed in on Joan's face as she said, "I was afraid," and ran out of the building.

"One of our finest moments," said Bingham. "Take away truth, and people will lie. Scoff at virtue, and betrayal becomes a matter of course."

"Then these techniques really work!" said a man in the audience.

"Absolutely," said Bingham. "*If* you'll pardon the expression." The audience laughed. "But it takes time, the right personalities, the right circumstances."

"So what about this young lady?" someone asked.

"Take away truth, and people will lie.
Scoff at virtue, and betrayal
becomes a matter of course."

"Mmm," said Bingham with a testy side-glance at Elisha. "This young lady and her brother." He nodded to the technician.

Elisha was stunned. Now she was watching Margaret Jones talk to her and Elijah at that same table in the same youth shelter. For all she knew, even the *soup* was the same.

"We chose these two because they *do* have a strong religious background and they *do* believe in absolutes. Our goal, of course, was to compare their reactions to the same situations, and see if their particular system of truth could be broken." With another sideways glance at Elisha, Bingham quipped, "And as we anticipated, it hasn't been easy."

Bingham nodded to the technician, and another video began to play on the big screen: Elijah and Elisha reciting the Ten Commandments in Booker's class; the two of them debating Mr. Easley; Elijah telling Booker, ". . . it's like you and I are from different planets or something. For you, it's all power and money. For me, it's God. It's Truth. I could never work for you . . ."; and Elisha surrounded by the kids in the Rec Center, telling Alex, "Jerry would have to bow to you. He'd have to say you're right, and he won't do that. And neither will I," and handing the scarf back to Cher.

The audience members groaned with dismay at every scene.

"No, no, be encouraged," said Bingham. "It's all data, useful in future research. For example . . ."

The technician cued another recording, and there, on the big screen, was a video of Elijah and Alex having their terrible fight, and a few instant replays of Elijah finally decking Alex with a high kick. The audience loved that.

"You'll notice how even a reasonable person can be reduced to brute force when truth and reason are no longer available."

"Ahh," said the audience, feeling better.

"But this is why we brought them here. Let's face it: Children of this type will always be our greatest challenge. They're difficult to deceive, they can't be programmed, they don't believe something if it isn't true, they don't put their own comfort before their sense of right and wrong, and worst of all, they actually think things through. As we have seen, discussion groups and consensus conditioning couldn't undermine this mentality, nor could peer pressure, nor could intimidation and fear. However . . ."

Bingham came closer to Elisha, eyeing her as if she were a rat in an experiment. "We have both of them in place for the final phase, and we're ready."

"But . . . ," Stern asked, jotting on his clipboard. "How do we factor in the fact that they—"

"Are undercover investigators?" Bingham asked. The audience rustled and murmured with alarm, but Bingham held up his hand. "It only sweetens the pie. That call she made will actually

Bingham came closer to Elisha, eyeing her as if she were a rat in an experiment.

be to our advantage, bringing all the birds into one snare, so to speak." He leaned on a control panel, looking gleefully at the young lady in the chair. "And judging from the condition of her brother . . ." He chuckled reassuringly. "In just a matter of hours, neither of them will be anything to worry about."

14

the mind maze

North Idaho was very scenic, but very frustrating if you wanted to get anywhere in a hurry—such as the tiny town of Stony Bend, deep in the St. Joe National Forest. The highway followed the St. Joe River, which meant it wandered, wiggled, and wound for mile after mile, with hills, curves, and blind corners that could not be driven too briskly if you wanted to arrive at all. Nate drove, Sarah slept, and then they traded, and finally, just before night turned to gray morning, they pulled into the town—what there was of it.

Stony Bend was still asleep. The local cafe was closed and dark. A few of the small, metal-roofed houses had porch lights on, but that was all. Some logging trucks were parked along the highway, loaded but going nowhere at the moment.

"Let's try that all-night gas station," said Nate, still waking up.

Sarah pulled in next to the pumps. "I'll fill the tank, if you want to go inside."

It was a typical quick-stop, a place to buy gas and a little bit of everything else. A ponderous woman was sitting behind the counter amid the beef jerky and chewing tobacco, smoking a cigarette and listening to a country music station.

"Good morning," said Nate.

"Hi there," she replied, crushing out her cigarette.

"I wonder if you could help me . . ."

Sarah used her credit card and started pumping the gas, watching Nate conversing with the big woman inside. The woman was listening, but now she was shaking her head, looking like she didn't know anything. Nate and Sarah had seen that response a lot since arriving in Idaho.

A pickup truck pulled in on the other side of the pumps, between Sarah and the store. Sarah had to move a little to one side to see how Nate was doing. He must have asked directions. The woman was pointing up the highway, scratching her head, reaching for a pen . . .

The driver of the pickup started pumping gas into his truck, leaning against the side of his truck, his eyes staring into the distance at nothing in particular. Sarah glanced at him—and moved quickly behind the pumping station, turning her back, stroking her forehead to conceal her face. *Hang on, girl. Don't freak out. Steady. Steady.*

Carefully, discretely, she edged around the pumping station just enough to catch a good look at the man's face. He was still staring off into the distance, waiting for his tank to fill. He was a little man with a round head and thin, black hair.

The clerk from the Dartmoor Hotel.

Get out here, Nate. Come on, get out here.

Even though her tank wasn't full, she hung up the nozzle, screwed on the gas cap, and jumped into the car, ready and waiting behind the wheel.

Clunk! The little man's tank was full. He hung up the nozzle and climbed into his cab.

Nate!

The pickup pulled out of the station. Nate was walking back, looking at some scribbled notes and looking around.

Sarah put the heel of her hand to the car horn and left it there. That got his attention. She gestured at him madly, and he ran.

Mr. Bingham turned toward the big screens. "The Maze."

All four screens combined to form one huge image, that of a tiny figure stumbling, staggering, arms covering his head, surrounded by a mad swirling of shapes, surfaces, colors, sounds, swept and tossed like a particle of lint in a cosmic washing machine.

Elisha bolted to her feet. "Elijah!"

The thin tech with the ponytail stepped in, gently touching her shoulder. "Please. Sit down. It'll be all right."

Elisha sat, her eyes glued to the big screens. Her brother fell, got up again, turned several circles, clamped his hands over his ears. "Stop it! STOP IT! What are you doing to him?"

Bingham nodded to a technician, who went to work at his console.

The horrible bedlam subsided. The colors faded. The noise quieted down. Elijah was now in a white fog, with nothing visible around him. He was standing still, dazed, staring, half-conscious—like Alvin Rogers.

Bingham began explaining to his audience, "This is a continuation of a previous experiment. As you recall, a breach in the system allowed our last subject to escape—most unfortunate!—but that problem was quickly contained, and now we have a replacement volunteer. The question before us: Can the human psyche really function in the absence of truth? How far can the mind go when nothing, nothing at all, can be known for certain?"

He looked at Elisha, checking her over, and then nodded to the techs sitting at all those consoles.

Lights came on around Elisha, making her jump.

Suddenly, she saw herself on the big screen, sitting in the same chair, except . . . she looked great. She was wearing a white blouse, a clean pair of jeans, some cool western jewelry, and a pair of boots beyond a Springfield budget. Her face was clean, her hair was neat, and she wasn't sitting in a strange little green alcove surrounded by lights—she was sitting quite comfortably in the family room of a huge log home. There was a large, stone fireplace behind her, soft living room furniture around her, a deep, wool rug on the floor. There was a weird, white fog in the room, but it was quickly dissolving away.

> "... The question before us: Can the human psyche really function in the absence of truth?..."

Elijah's ears were ringing and his head was spinning, but for now, for this one brief moment, the ride was over. He was weak and trembling, hunched over. His hands were shaking. He'd already thrown up a third time and his stomach felt like it would never hold food again, but at least the floor, the ground, the haze, the bog, the water, the sand, *whatever* it was under his feet, had stopped moving. The white fog around him was clearing. He thought he saw a wool rug below him, and then . . . a wall made of logs . . . a soft couch . . . a crackling fire in a stone fireplace.

Was he still alive? It was so hard to think, to place one thought after another.

"Elijah," came a lovely voice, like an angel. He knew that voice. "Elijah."

He saw his sister, seated in a comfortable chair, smiling at him.

"Sis?" he asked, his voice hoarse from screaming.

"It's all right, Elijah," she said. "Come and sit down. Take a load off."

He hobbled forward, comforted by her smiling, serene face, by the warmth of the lovely room. This had to be real. He wanted very much for it to be real. "Is this heaven?"

"It's anything you want it to be."

He sank onto the couch, then reclined, his head sinking into the soft pillows.

"It feels great to finally rest, doesn't it?"

He could only sigh a deep, tired sigh and nod his head.

"So just . . . just let go."

Even with his mind mangled, Elijah still found a tiny spark of curiosity. "Let go of what?"

"The struggle. Trying to know. That's where all the pain comes from, Elijah: trying to believe that some things are true. Life is so much easier when you don't have to worry about truth."

———

"That lying little imp!" Elisha said to herself as she watched herself on the screen. "Elijah, don't believe her!"

So the whole thing was a hologram, an incredibly realistic, three-dimensional projection! That explained the mysterious image of her brother that lured her into this place. She looked around her, above her. For the first time, she noticed a camera lens pointing down at her from the ceiling. These clever people were recording her image as she sat in the chair, enhancing it with all their fancy computers, and reassembling it in front of her maze-dazed brother, making it tell the most outrageous lies.

I've got to get through to him!

———

Nate and Sarah followed the pickup to a slightly sagging little cabin off a side road. By now, they were more than ready for a direct approach. Sarah walked right up on the front porch and gave the front door several sharp raps.

The little man opened the door, plainly curious and annoyed. "Yes?"

"Hi. Sorry to disturb you so early in the morning. I was wondering, have you seen a boy and a girl around here, both sixteen, good looking, like their mother?"

He started to shake his head. "No, I haven't—" But then he got a good look at her.

She confirmed it for him. "You're right! You know me from somewhere!"

"I, I don't think so."

"Sure. The Dartmoor Hotel in Seattle. You were the desk clerk, remember?"

He started to close the door. "I'm busy—"

She kicked the door, hurling it open and hurling him a good distance, too. "Or maybe it was the Light of Day Youth Shelter. I get the two confused."

He was about to argue further, but there was an angry mama bear coming into his house, and while she was not *overly* hefty, she was not petite, either. He turned and ran through the cabin and out the back door—where Nate was waiting for him and

She confirmed it for him. "You're right! You know me from somewhere!"

quickly slammed him face-first against the back wall, holding him there in an inescapable armlock. "Now we can make this really simple. You have our kids and we want them." He gave the little man another slam against the wall. "Your turn."

"I don't know what you're talking about!"

Another slam. "Wrong answer."

A voice behind them ordered, "Let him go, Springfield."

There was a tall, imposing man standing in the backyard, one hand tucked inside his suit jacket.

Sarah and Nate froze, but Nate didn't let go.

"Easy now," said the man. "We're on the same side." He pulled some ID from his jacket pocket and showed it to them. "The name's Nelson Farmer. I'm with the Bureau for Missing Children. I've been on this case since your children disappeared."

"Nelson Farmer," Sarah repeated thoughtfully.

"So who's *this* guy?" Nate demanded.

"One of the people we're after. You're right. He's a front man for the Knight-Moore project, and we're in the same boat as you are: There are kids missing and we want to know what he knows. Now just take it easy and let him go."

There was a wooden bench on the back porch. Nate put the man there, keeping an eye on him.

Sarah approached Nelson Farmer. "What do you know about our kids? Where are they?"

Farmer stepped forward, reaching inside his jacket again. "We're clearing up the details right now—"

"NOOO!" Sarah grabbed his arm, forcing it skyward.

His hand was holding a gun.

Nate was there in an instant, but Sarah already had Farmer in a very painful armhold, and with a skillful judo move she threw him to the ground. In less than a second, Farmer was looking up into the barrel of his own gun, now in Sarah's hand.

Nate smiled and gave a little nod. He never doubted.

"I've had someone pull a gun on me before," Sarah told Farmer, "and that's what it looked like."

Nate caught a movement out of the corner of his eye.

The little man was gone; the bush at the corner of the cabin was still wiggling where he'd passed.

"Be right back." Nate took off after him. He cleared the corner of the cabin and saw the man disappearing around the front. Close enough to catch, Nate figured, pouring on the speed. He heard a cry of pain and a scuffle as he came around the front of the cabin, then came face-to-face with four big guys in green jackets with big yellow letters on the front: U.S. MARSHAL. The little man was dangling from their strong arms.

Sarah thought the marines had arrived. More deputy marshals began flooding the backyard, guns ready. "Sarah Springfield?" asked one.

"Yes."

"Sorry we're late."

They had Farmer. She handed over Farmer's gun.

"He was going to kill you just as he killed Alvin Rogers," said a familiar voice coming around the cabin, "which would have repaired the breach in secrecy—except for the children, of course." It was Morgan, walking with Nate. "Your little hotel clerk was simply a decoy to lure you here."

"To a secluded place with no witnesses," said Nate.

"Exactly. You would have disappeared without a trace. Hello, Sarah. As for your red-headed woman, she is actually a Ms. Marian Winger, a longtime confidante and associate of Mr. Farmer there. Once cornered, she was very cooperative, and warned us that Mr. Farmer was following you. Since we knew where you were, we knew where Mr. Farmer would be." They strode right up to Farmer, now on his stomach as a marshal handcuffed him. Morgan spoke to Nate, but also for Farmer's benefit. "He's been taking advantage of a sacred trust: using his position and the files at the Bureau for Missing Children to screen and recruit runaways for experimentation. Ms. Winger was acting as his field agent, and she gave us all the details." Morgan knelt beside the

"He was going to kill you just as he killed Alvin Rogers," said a familiar voice coming around the cabin, "which would have repaired the breach in secrecy— except for the children, of course."

handcuffed Farmer. "And now, Mr. Farmer, you will tell us exactly where the children are."

――――――――

The perfect, heavenly Elisha leaned forward, her eyes intense. "It doesn't mean you can't believe something. No, it's even better than that: You can believe *anything*, anything you want, because if you believe it, that makes it true."

Elijah could only rest his head on the pillow and close his eyes as his sister went on and on.

". . . I love being able to create my own reality. I can be what I want, do what I want, believe what I want, and I don't have to worry about what God thinks . . ."

He was disappointed. After all he'd been through, he was actually hoping this was heaven. He was even hoping this was really his sister. Now his jumbled mind was beginning to put a few pieces together: If there was no reality, then he certainly couldn't count on there being a heaven; if nothing was really true, then even what this girl was saying wasn't true; if this girl really believed what she was saying, she wasn't his sister. All this left him with a discouraging conclusion: He was still in the middle of a waking nightmare and he was probably going crazy.

Tap, tap, tatap, tap tap . . .

What was that sound? He cracked one eye open. The pretty girl was still talking, her eyes focused somewhere across the room and not on him. His eye was drawn to her right hand, resting on the arm of the chair. Her fingers were drumming out a little rhythm, over and over again.

Elisha watched the big screen on the wall, trying to look as amazed and distraught as before as she drummed her fingers on the arm of her chair. God was answering her prayer: The other Elisha, while droning on and on about there being no truth, was drumming her fingers the very same way. The computer had picked it up as just a mannerism and sent it through to the phony image.

Mr. Bingham's eyes were glued to the big screen, and his voice squeaked a little with nervous anticipation. "Theoretically, his mind should be adequately erased by this point, ready to receive

> "Theoretically, his mind should be adequately erased by this point, ready to receive the input from what he thinks is his sister. If this works, we will have broken the last barrier to global control."

the input from what he thinks is his sister. If this works, we will have broken the last barrier to global control."

A man in the audience asked, "And what if it doesn't work?"

Mr. Bingham kept watching the screen as he answered. "That would be unthinkable. If it is the truth that sets people free, then we can't allow people to have it or even believe in it. They must follow, do, and believe what *we* say, or we cannot enslave them."

"Unthinkable," the man in the audience agreed.

Now everyone watched the screen with all the more interest and anxiety.

And Elisha kept tapping away, sending the same message.

———

"Truth is just what you make it, whatever you want it to be, and no matter what you choose, it isn't wrong if you sincerely feel it . . ."

Elijah closed his eyes and tried to block out the girl's endless ramblings. He was listening to those finger taps, the only thing that made sense.

It was code. Springfield code: O R 6 O C L O C K . . . P R O J E C T O R 6 O C L O C K . . . P R O J E . . .

Then again, maybe it wasn't code. Maybe it was just silly rhythms that he was making into code in his poor, tired mind.

But the letters kept repeating, like an endless loop, the same number of seconds every time.

Same number of seconds. Same length of time. Repeating pattern. A rhythm, a beat, a pulse.

Whoa, hold on, hold on.

He knew this pulse, this beat. For the past eternity of chaos, he'd been living in it. It was everywhere. The *rushing, rushing, rushing* of the wind, the *throbbing, throbbing, throbbing* of the ground, the *swaying, swaying, swaying* of the trees, the rhythm of the rooms, the halls, the colors. It all kept time to this beat, like a big clock ticking, like a machine running, around and around, over and over. He could feel it like the beating of his own heart, like it was a part of him.

"They're at the gate!" shouted Easley, switching one of the monitor screens to a shot of the big iron gate.

Everyone in the room gasped, leaned forward, watched in awe.

Almost every kid on the campus was there, an angry mob of nearly fifty, armed with axes, picks, rakes, shovels, banging, prying, bashing, digging away at the gate.

**But the letters kept repeating,
like an endless loop, the same
number of seconds every time.**

Bingham was impressed. "Nearly all of them, and so early in the morning!" He turned to the audience. "You see? After four years of research, we can now choose our raw materials, create the right circumstances, and in less than two weeks produce a dictator and his followers!"

The audience applauded. It was apparently a great moment.

Bingham mused to himself, "This 'Alexander' could have done very well as a global dictator." He laughed. "And I think he knows it, too. Why else would he choose such a name?"

"How long do we keep them there?" asked a technician.

"Stand by for closing procedure," Bingham answered. He turned to the thin guy in black. "Begin shutdown and evacuation." The man hurried from the room. Red lights began to flash overhead. Bingham turned to the audience. "We are reaching the end of the experiment. Please prepare to evacuate at any moment."

The audience began to stir around in the dark, shuffling papers, opening and closing briefcases, grabbing coats.

Elisha was watching her image. Her entire message wasn't getting through, only the little part about the projector, repeating over and over. The computer must have hit a glitch or something. Her plan wasn't working. "Mr. Bingham!"

He was quite occupied. Teachers and technicians were starting

Her plan wasn't working.

to scramble everywhere. Some of the equipment was closing down, the red and amber lights blinking out, the whirring of the processors going silent. At the far end of the room, a door slid open and the audience, faces still in the dark, began heading for it.

"Mr. Bingham! When are you going to let my brother out of there?"

Bingham watched the screen, then said over his shoulder, "When I know what I want to know, of course."

"You mean, when *you* can know, and *he* can't!"

Bingham actually smiled at her. "Brilliant!"

Elijah was counting seconds. One, two, three . . . up to six. Every time, six seconds. The loop, the pulse, the wave, was six seconds. When he closed his eyes and listened to the room, he could even hear the sound of the air recycle every six seconds. The girl, still talking, seemed to take a little breath every six seconds. Wow. In all this mess, he could *know* something, a sweet six seconds.

So what about the code those fingers kept tapping out? Maybe he could know that, too. CKPROJECTOR6OCLO . . . JECTOR6OCLOCK . . . PROJECTOR 6 OCLOCK.

Six o'clock. Did she mean, *behind* him? Projector behind him? He opened his eyes and looked toward the ceiling, then over the back of the couch.

He didn't see anything. Not yet.

Teachers and techs were wheeling large cases of equipment and data on hand trucks, moving it all out that open door at the end of the room. It was all going like clockwork, well rehearsed. The audience remained in the shadows by the door, watching the final seconds of the great experiment on the big screens.

"All right," said Bingham, "let them in."

The tech threw a switch, and with a loud creak and groan, the iron gate broke open. Alexander and his mob were jubilant, waving their tools in the air. "Let's go!" Alexander yelled, and the whole mob moved forward, through the gate and up the walk.

"Any stragglers?" Bingham asked.

Mrs. Meeks looked up from her console. "Warren's friends are hanging back. Warren is still in his room, not wanting to be seen. We still have Tom Cruise and his two friends hiding near the Dumpsters and a few kids hiding in the buildings."

"Let's contain them."

Meeks held down a talk switch and spoke into her headset. "Begin containment."

"Demolition? Report."

The third tech down the row reported, "Dozers in position, charges armed."

Bingham smiled—again. "I've grown to love this part!"

Overhead, there was a faint pounding. An image appeared on one of the big screens: the front door of the mansion. Alexander and the mob had reached it and were trying to break it in.

"Let them work at it a while. Let them have a feeling of accomplishment." He thought that last line was funny, and laughed.

"Mr. Bingham!" Easley shouted, pointing to the other screen.

Every eye in the place went to that screen. There were audible gasps.

Even Elisha gasped and her heart went sick.

Her brother Elijah had become a madman. He was singing, jumping, dancing around the room, hiding behind the chair where the phony Elisha sat, then jumping up, then hiding again, circling, ranting, and raving.

Bingham hurried closer to the screen. "More sound, please."

Easley reached for a knob on his console and turned up the volume.

Elijah was singing, "I've got a brain, and you've got a brain, and it's so much pain! I've got a brain, and you've got a brain, and it's so much *poop!*" Then he laughed and started ranting, "Gobbledee gobbledee gobbledee gobbledee gobbledee gook!

> Elijah was singing, "I've got a brain, and you've got a brain, and it's so much pain! I've got a brain, and you've got a brain, and it's so much poop!"

Gobbledee gobbledee gobbledee gobbledee gobbledee *geek!*"
Then he rolled on the floor, kicking his feet in the air, then spun
in sideways circles, pedaling against the floor with his feet.

Now Bingham roared with laughter, so much it made him
wheeze.

Easley reached up and shook his hand. "Congratulations."

Booker came over and did the same. "Congratulations."

"Very good, very good!" said Bingham. "So these people can
be broken after all! Make sure we get a full record of the data."

"My brother . . . ," said Elisha, her spirit collapsing in sorrow.
"My sweet brother . . ."

"All right," said Bingham. "Open the door and let's be done
with it." A tech threw another switch, and the front door of the
mansion caved in. "Be sure they all go inside."

The screens combined into one big composite and switched
to an interior shot of . . . what in the world was it?

To Elisha, it looked like Alexander and his mob were pouring
into a huge warehouse, a vast empty shell, and from the looks on
their faces, they were as stunned and perplexed as she was. She
strained to understand what she was seeing: bare, white walls,
expansive concrete floor, high windows—yes, but no rooms, no
stairs, no furniture, nothing!

The mansion on the hill, that huge, foreboding structure
that had all the kids in awe; that mysterious citadel where
power resided; that symbol of ultimate authority and rulership,
was a fake.

An empty shell.

A big nothing.

"Everyone's inside," reported the tech.

"Seal them in," said Bingham.

The tech threw a switch, and on the screen, the front and side doors of the empty shell suddenly disappeared as huge panels slammed into place. The kids started screaming.

Bingham looked at Elisha and told his crew, "Throw her in with the others."

15

veritas

Farmer wasn't smiling, but his arrogance showed clearly enough. He wasn't about to say anything.

"You have an amazing sense of loyalty, Mr. Farmer," said Morgan, turning away. "I wish you were working for us instead of them."

The hotel clerk was sitting on the wooden bench on the back porch, handcuffed to a bench leg, a federal marshal on either side of him. He didn't look nearly as arrogant or confident as Farmer did, and Nate noticed.

"So what's going to happen to Mr. Farmer?" Nate asked.

Morgan whistled at the thought of it. "Pretty serious charges. There are laws protecting schoolchildren from invasive psychological questioning or conditioning, and I would say Mr. Farmer has conspired with his friends to violate every one of them—not to mention his role in kidnapping the children, plus the murder of Alvin Rogers and the attempted murders of you and Sarah."

"Which doesn't look good for anyone who helped him."

Morgan looked at the hotel clerk as he answered. "No, especially if anything happens to those children. Even if someone were hired simply as a stooge, as a decoy, if harm came to even one of the children, that person could face the same charges as an accessory."

The little clerk was clearly shaken by that, looking at Morgan, then at Farmer, then at Morgan.

"However, if such a person were to help us save the children from any harm, that would certainly change the picture for the better."

The little man was shaking, but remained silent.

―――――

Mr. Bingham threw some papers into his briefcase and fastened it shut. "Leave Mr. Springfield in the Maze while the computer finishes the program. An apt closure, don't you think?"

On his way to join the others going out the door, he stopped by Elisha's little TV stage. "So I imagine you've learned what it is you came to learn, but of course, like yourself, that knowledge is only temporary. After today, the Knight-Moore Academy will cease to exist, even as a memory, and your investigation will be moot. But make no mistake: What we've learned here will definitely live on—in schools, in films, on television, in recordings, in textbooks—and my friends and I will simply wait. After all, when the world does fall into chaos, such as we've demonstrated here, *someone* will have to take charge, won't they?"

"It'll be all about power," said Elisha.

"And *we* will have it," said Bingham with a wink. "Good-bye."

Bingham crossed the room and disappeared through the door.

The thin technician with the ponytail came over to Elisha, said, "I'm very sorry," and threw a lever.

With a neck-wrenching spin, the whole platform where Elisha was sitting rotated until she was facing the wall behind her. A panel in the wall opened, the platform pitched forward, and Elisha tumbled into a tight, elevator-sized cavity.

It *was* an elevator. It lurched upward, rotated, came to a stomach-turning halt, opened, pitched forward, and threw her out.

There were shouts and squeals of alarm. "It's Sally!" "Where did she come from?" "Is that the way out of here?"

She looked up from the floor and saw Britney, Melinda, Ramon, Tom Cruise, and so many others gathering around her, their faces longing for answers. "What's happening, Sally?" "Where are we?" "What's going to happen?"

The elevator was gone, of course, hidden behind a panel that closed immediately. She got to her feet, looking at all the frightened faces looking back at her, all the kids of different sizes, shapes, colors, and backgrounds, clothing askew, hands and faces dirty from the big struggle with the gate and the front door.

> "There were guards. Security people, I guess. They rounded up everybody. We're all here."

Warren stepped forward, still blotchy with white paint, and extended his hand. "Glad you're okay, Sally."

She appreciated his handshake. "So they got you, too."

Warren nodded, exchanging a glance with Tom Cruise and the other kids who weren't here by choice. "There were guards. Security people, I guess. They rounded up everybody. We're all here."

Nearby was Brett, standing in the middle of the vast room, exploring the white, featureless walls with frightened eyes, looking helpless. Rory and his big gang of toughs were clustered together, looking scared—they wouldn't be slugging and bullying their way out of this problem.

At the far end of the room, standing alone and looking very small in this huge, empty shell of a house, was "Alexander." Elisha took a good, long look at him, for the picture spoke volumes. So this was Alexander, the great leader, and this was his mighty revolution! He had made it to the top, to the pinnacle of power. He'd taken the mansion.

And the mansion was empty.

"My name isn't Sally," she said. "It's Elisha Springfield. Jerry's real name is Elijah, and he's my brother. And I guess you've figured it out: This whole thing was one big lie, and *Harold Carlson* hasn't conquered anything."

Harold "Alexander" Carlson just stood there, speechless, crestfallen, staring at the walls while his followers stared at him. He had no orders to give, no new visions for the future.

BOOM! An explosion, close enough to shake the floor!

They ran to the windows and could see a ball of fire and bil-lowing smoke where dorm A once stood. At the very edge of the campus, a huge yellow bulldozer was rumbling and squeaking onto the field.

———

"OOOH!" The sound of a faraway explosion totally rattled the little man. He jumped from the bench, jerked back by the hand-cuff around his wrist. "Okay! Okay! Nobody hired me to take a rap for murder. I was just supposed to sit there in the hotel in case anybody came in asking questions. I didn't know—"

"Be quiet!" Farmer yelled. They were his first words since being arrested.

"I didn't know they were going to kill the kids, I swear!"

Nate, Sarah, and Morgan closed in on the frightened man. "Keep going," said Nate, and it was far more threat than request.

"They never killed the kids before. All the other times, all the other years, they were signing up kids who volunteered. They had the kids for two weeks and then the kids went home and everything was okay, no problem, nobody asking questions, nothing." He took a breath, his eyes searching the ground. "I should have suspected something when they started signing up runaways, kids who were already missing."

Nate took hold of both his shoulders and locked eyes with him. "What are you saying?"

"It's the fifth year, the last experiment. I don't know what they're doing up there, but this time they have to erase every-thing—not just the campus. I mean the kids, *everything*."

"How do we get there?"

"The road's gone. They took that out yesterday. There's a tunnel . . ."

It was all Nate could do to keep from crushing the answer out of the man. "WHERE?"

The man rattled the handcuff. "I'll take you there, just let me loose!"

Elijah was getting toward the end of his strength, singing crazily, jumping suddenly, trying to be unpredictable, but his theory was proving out.

Whenever he paused to rest, the warm, welcoming environment of the family room of a big log house surrounded him like a fluffy comforter, steady, stable, and unchanging. The girl in the chair kept right on smiling and babbling, her fingers still tapping away the same little coded message.

Whenever he acted crazy, doing new, unpredictable behaviors, the environment got sketchy, the textures foggy, the sensory illusions of smell, touch, and sound dull.

Most of all, the whole world froze for a minuscule moment every six seconds, like clockwork.

So Elijah realized he could still *know* things, and what he knew right now was that the computer running this mad ride was reloading and processing information on a six-second cycle, a fact he could detect only because he'd been in this place for so long he could hear it and feel it.

As long as everything happened predictably, like one step following another, an exhale following an inhale, a scratch following an itch, the computer could handle it.

But if he gave the computer new information it wasn't expecting—silly songs with the last word changed or not rhyming when it should, or goofy antics that weren't predictable—then the computer had to process all that new information, which took time, and this horrible, crazy world would actually *blink*, just for an instant, every six seconds.

It was that blink he was watching for as he made a blithering fool of himself, and after several crazy, exhausting cycles, he knew when to expect it, like dancing to the rhythm of music. His dear sister was right; behind the couch where he'd been lying, where usually he saw only a wall of huge logs, the round shape of a lens would flash into view, quick like the click of a shutter, every six seconds.

The projector, at six o'clock.

"Okay," he said to himself and anyone listening, "one more time."

He jumped to one side of the girl's chair, then back, then back where he started, and then—jumped in place, whooping out a stupid song he hoped the computer hadn't heard before—"Back up the batter and *Whoof!* In the flutter and wowie, look at us bang on the roof!"—it all had to be new information!

The wall blinked after six seconds. He saw the lens. He hopped, went to his knees and clucked, stood up again, spun in a circle—

The wall blinked again. Now he was sure where the lens was, even if he couldn't see it.

He grabbed the chair the girl was sitting in and yanked it high over his head. The girl remained exactly where she was, sitting in midair, still smiling at him and telling him he could create his own truth any way he wanted it.

With all his strength, and quite glad about it, he brought the chair down where the projector was hiding and felt the chair connect with something. There was a crash and the tinkling of glass. The girl sitting in midair began to flutter, her voice turned to static, and then, like a flame blown out, she vanished.

Now all *this* was new information, too. The pleasant family room was looking foggy, out of focus, and within six seconds Elijah caught sight of a *real* wall beyond the log wall—and the steel rungs of a ladder.

He ran forward, arms outstretched, eyes locked open to see the next blink.

There were the rungs again, embedded in the wall just two feet to the left, within reach!

His hand locked onto a steel rung that wasn't there.

He closed his eyes, tried not to feel the room he was in, tried to sense only the ladder—

His hand locked onto a steel rung that wasn't there.

No! It is there! The ladder is real! Climb, Elijah! Climb, no matter what your senses tell you!

He pulled on the rung. Somewhere inside his nervous system, a faint message was delivered: You're lifting yourself. All around, on every side, he was still in that pleasant family room in the big log house and nothing had changed; but he groped, then he grabbed another unseen, almost unfelt rung, and pulled again. Now his toe found a rung, and he pushed with his leg.

He was climbing out of there, no matter what the room said, no matter what he thought he was seeing.

BOOM! Another explosion rattled the valley, the shock wave bounding off the mountainsides and rolling through again, shaking the ground and quivering the mansion. Elisha and all the kids could only watch helplessly as dorm B blossomed toward the sky in a cloud of smoke, fire, and splinters.

"They're erasing the campus," said Elisha. "They're going to cover up everything they did here."

Warren was beside her, looking out the same window. "So what are they going to do with us?"

Elisha couldn't say it. She didn't even want to think it. "Can we break these windows?"

"We've tried."

"Let's try again."

Even an ax in Rory's hands simply bounced off the thick Plexiglas.

Warren called out, "Okay, everybody, *do* something! Grab a tool and do some damage, find a weak spot, a crack, a door, anything!"

Even Alexander complied, grabbing a shovel and looking for any seam or crack he might be able to pry open.

BOOM! There went the main classroom building, all of Ms. Fitzhugh's artwork, all the foreign language materials, all the history and social studies books. Ashes, fragments of desks, and tattered pages floated through the air like snowflakes.

———

Nate and Sarah could hear the explosion, even feel it in their feet as they followed the little hotel clerk through the woods to a narrow tunnel hewn and blasted out of the rock.

"Looks like nothing but an old mine," said a marshal.

"It used to be a mine entrance," said the little man, "but they bored it out to use as an escape tunnel. They had this whole thing planned from the beginning."

"So how do we know you're not bluffing?"

BOOM . . . OOM . . . OOM . . . oom . . . oom . . . This time the sound of the explosion came echoing at them through the tunnel.

"Sounds like this will get us there," said Nate, clicking on a flashlight. They'd all been advised they would need lights.

The marshal waved to his men. "Okay, Wyrick, Perkins, Bocelli, up front with me. Springfields and Morgan, stay close behind. Hanson, stay here with the suspect. The rest of you take up the rear." Then he reached into his belt and produced a spare semiautomatic pistol, handing it to Nate. "You may need this."

Nate received it. "Thanks."

They plunged into the black, endless throat of the tunnel.

―――――――

Elijah kept going through the motions, clinging with desperate hope to each rung of the ladder, hoping the faint sensations of gripping and climbing were the correct ones. The pleasant room around him was starting to warp and ripple as the colors, sounds, and even smells, became . . . *less real.* He kept going, grabbing and pulling, stepping and pushing, rung after rung—

His head broke into the clear, suddenly, as if he'd just broken through the surface of a lake. Though his body was still floundering in a swirling, fluttering nonreality, groping to find the next rung, from the neck up, the world was real. He could see cables and wiring, a vast steel gridwork supporting lights, holographic projectors, movable walls and panels, color and sound generators. It looked like the most expensive movie sound stage ever built.

He could clearly see the rungs of the ladder now, embedded in the concrete wall he was climbing, and directly above him, a catwalk. He pulled himself out of the swirling light, out of the weird, fuzzy static until, like a drowning man flopping into a boat, he rolled onto the catwalk. Below him, the pleasant family room, several disjointed hallways, even some phony forest, wavered and rippled as if they were under water.

He'd had enough of this place. There was a door at the far end of the catwalk. He pulled himself to his feet, then limped and staggered through that door.

He was in a control room, most likely the place where they concocted and controlled his continuous, mind-frying hell. Strangely, the place was deserted. Only a few consoles and monitors were still operating. The sound of frantic voices and clanging tools was coming from somewhere, like a video playing. He dragged himself farther into the room, looking about, trying to find the source. His eye caught a glimmer of light behind him—

He turned to see huge screens on the wall, and immediately recognized his sister and most of the student body, all banging, gouging, prying with garden tools, trying to get out of a huge, white room with high windows.

His mind was tired. He watched them struggle, but nothing connected; nothing made any sense.

His mind was tired. He watched them struggle, but nothing connected; nothing made any sense.

Then one piece fell into place: Those windows look like the mansion's windows.

Next piece: It's the mansion.

Final piece: They're trapped inside!

Immediately below the screens, a computer monitor flickered, running through columns and graphics. He stumbled to it, stared at it. It meant nothing to him. *What . . . what is this?*

There were lines of information in bright red: DORMITORY A . . . DORMITORY B . . . MAIN CLASSROOM . . . LIBRARY. To the left of each line, four zeroes and the flashing word DONE.

Below these were the rest of the campus structures, all listed in green, preceded by four digits and the word STANDBY. The numbers before DORMITORY C were counting down, just going through 410.8 and dropping fast.

At the very bottom was the line, 055.5__STANDBY__ MANSION AND CONTROL CENTER.

Elijah sat at the console, staring at the monitor, then studying the big screens above. One showed the kids trapped in the mansion; another showed a burning pile of rubble and a black column of smoke. A third showed a dormitory—with the letter C on the corner.

Was all this supposed to mean something? He just kept staring, his mind an exhausted, burned-out blob inside his head.

Elisha was banging with an ax on the seam of the front door, guessing where a hinge or a latch might be, but the structure was solid, her desperate blows futile.

Rory came along. "Let me try."

She stood back, and he struck the seam so hard it broke the ax handle. He threw the broken end down and just stared.

"There has to be a way," she said.

Rory looked at her a moment, then said, "I want you to know, I really did like your brother."

BOOM! This time it was dorm C. Beyond the smoke and flame they could see another bulldozer standing by.

———

Elijah saw the explosion on the big screen, and then—

He saw the line "DORMITORY C" go from green to red. The numbers were all zeroes, and the computer reported with the flashing word DONE.

He stared another moment, and then . . .

Oh, great . . .

It finally sank in: The computer was executing a program, setting off charges to destroy all the buildings—with *this* building the last on the list.

Elijah could see the exit door, still open. He could still get out of here. He could also see his sister and classmates struggling, crying, trying to get out of the mansion.

I won't leave you here, Elisha.

He remained seated at the console, staring at the monitor, praying he could figure out how in the world to abort the program. His mind just wasn't clicking.

"Dear Lord Jesus, I need your help—uh, right now. I mean, *really* right now. *Please.*"

The tunnel went straight through the mountain for hundreds of feet, maybe thousands. There didn't seem to be an end to it.

"Heads up," said the marshal.

There were faint lights coming the other way. *Click-clack!* Nate heard the marshals chambering rounds in their pistols. He did the same.

"Escapees, no doubt," Morgan nearly whispered.

They quickened their pace, nearly running, half blind in the dark, heading for those lights. The lights began to waver, dart about. They heard distant, echoing voices of alarm.

Ping PaPing! A bullet ricocheted off the rock walls while everyone ducked. *BANGangangangangang!!!* The sound of the shot echoed up and down the tunnel. The lights reversed. The "escapees" were turning tail and running.

"Let's go! Let's go! Let's GO!" hollered the marshal.

OOOM . . . oom . . . oom . . . oom. Another explosion, much closer, much louder.

Britney and Cher both screamed, covering their ears as they huddled in a corner, totally beside themselves. Alexander banged on the stubborn Plexiglas with both fists, roaring in total panic.

Elisha, Rory, and Warren watched through a window as the last dorm building disintegrated in a ball of fire.

"They're going to blow up everything, aren't they?" said Rory.

"Even this building," Warren added.

From all she had seen and heard in the control room, Elisha could only reach one conclusion. "Yes. I believe they are."

The clanging of the tools was beginning to subside. The kids were starting to give up.

Elisha felt a hand on her shoulder. It was Joan, all tears. Neither had to say a word; Elisha just held Joan close as Joan wept in remorse.

Another explosion! The concussion pounded the mansion like a drum. The kids flinched, cried, screamed.

The Rec Center was gone, and all the games were reduced to black, burning ash adrift in the wind.

Elijah kept staring at the screen, trying to get his mind to grab hold of something: *Okay, red means the building's blown, green means it's going to be blown, the numbers counting down mean the number of seconds and tenths of seconds before each blast . . .*

There was a field labeled RESET. He clicked on that, but got an error message: PLEASE ENTER RESET QUANTITY.

Reset quantity, reset quantity . . . what quantity?

He stared at the columns of numbers not yet counting down. *Come on, come on, what's the relationship? How did they stack the numbers?*

Oh, Lord, don't let it be a logarithm, not today.

———

The Campus Exchange billowed into the sky, a cloud of splinters, pulverized stone, and shredded Knight-Moore sports clothing and souvenirs.

Nate and Sarah heard the explosion just before they broke out of the tunnel into the daylight, and now they could see the smoke through the trees, filling the valley below. The marshals fanned out, giving chase to unknown people—men and women in business attire carrying briefcases and valises, running in all directions through the forest. By the way those people were struggling, slipping, and tripping through the brush in their dress shoes and high heels, it seemed they wouldn't get far.

A trail led from the tunnel entrance, and up ahead, through the trees, Nate, Sarah, and Morgan could see the towering white walls of a huge mansion. They ran for it.

BOOM! Another structure went up in a ball of fire and smoke.

They heard bulldozers in the valley, scraping, rolling, squeaking.

Morgan started crashing down the hill through the trees, shouting at the marshals, "Stop those bulldozers! Stop them!"

Then Nate and Sarah heard something else: a low, close-to-the-ground snuffling, then a snorting. Some bushes rustled. Some twigs snapped.

Nate raised his pistol, aiming it in the direction of the noise.

There was a growl, the pounding of big feet. They saw a large, furry form charging through the brush, and then a monstrous head appeared, a roaring bear with glistening teeth.

Nate fired two rounds, then a third.

Sparks exploded from the bear's mouth and chest, and then, a stream of smoke. The big creature began to jerk and jolt like a poorly driven car, until finally it burst out of the bushes and lurched to a stop only a few yards away, hissing and smoking, the growl reduced to garbled radio noise. There was a smell like burning wire. Hydraulic fluid dribbled out on the ground. This bear had steel wheels on his feet.

No time to wonder about it. They ran on.

They saw a large, furry form charging through the brush, and then a monstrous head appeared, a roaring bear with glistening teeth.

The computer monitor was telling Elijah that the cafeteria had just blown up. The numbers next to OFFICE were counting down now. When they dropped down to a certain value, the office building was going to blow.

What value?

He went to the bottom of the list—just three lines down, now—and checked out the building where he and the other kids were this very moment. *Hey! 55.5 seconds! That has to be the demolition cycle, 55.5 seconds!*

He entered that from the keyboard.

ERROR. PLEASE ENTER RESET QUANTITY.

"There's somebody out there!" Jamal shouted, and all the kids ran to the windows.

"There goes somebody else!" said Rory.

Elisha could see green-jacketed marshals running across the front lawn. The kids raised a ruckus, banging on the windows, yelling, screaming.

Alexander yelled like a wild man, banging and swearing, but to no avail.

The marshals kept going.

"They can't hear us!" Elisha moaned.

Alexander yelled like a wild man, banging and swearing, but to no avail.

Then, suddenly, Elisha saw a vision like a flash of reality, like a bolt from the ordinary, real world piercing this nightmare.

She saw her mom and dad running toward the mansion, searching all around the grounds with their eyes, trying to find any sign—

Elisha screamed as she'd never screamed before. "It's my mom and dad!"

Hope flooded that big white prison. The kids pressed against the windows, waving, straining for a glimpse, longing to see a real mom and dad out there.

Sarah heard some faint noises, looked, and it was like seeing the heavens opened. There was Elisha, trapped behind the glass. "Nate! Nate, it's Elisha!"

She leaped up on the porch, went to the window, and put her hand against the thick Plexiglas. Elisha, crying unashamedly, pressed her palm against her mother's, the glass between them.

Nate tried the front door. It was sealed shut, like it was part of the wall. "What about the windows?"

Sarah replied, "Unbreakable, probably bulletproof."

The sound of a big machine echoed up from the valley. "I'll be right back." Nate took off down the walkway toward the big open gate.

KABOOM! The office building was history.

Elijah was talking out loud to himself, trying to get his brain to work. "Okay, 55.5, 55.5 . . . Okay, yeah, increments of 55.5 . . . okay, twice that is 111 . . ."

The computer was telling him there was only one more building to blow up before it was time to blow up *this* one.

"Okay, reset, reset . . . two buildings to go, we're counting down from 111 . . ."

He entered 111.

ERROR. PLEASE ENTER RESET QUANTITY.

With some help from an armed U.S. marshal, Nate bumped the nearest bulldozer operator from his machine and took over. He put the big monster in high gear, opened the throttle, and crossed the field like an army tank. The gate was already broken open; he had only to widen the opening as he crashed through.

BOOM! The last remaining structure on the campus went up like a volcano.

Sirens began shrieking in the control room. Strobes began to flash. Elijah had only one green line left, and it was counting down, 55 seconds . . . 45 . . . 35 . . .

All right, Elijah, think! THINK!

55.5 increments, twice is 111 . . . that doesn't work . . .

Nate was rolling, thundering, screeching up the walkway, heading for the mansion, looking for the best place to ram a hole. He gestured wildly to Sarah and yelled, "Get the kids back!"

Sarah waved through the window, "Get back! Get back!"

The kids inside ran to the farthest corner, dragging any kids too hysterical to move on their own.

25 seconds.

Okay. Twelve buildings, twelve lines . . . twelve times 55.5 . . .

Elijah couldn't do it in his head. The sirens were jumbling what was left of his brain. He looked for some paper and a pencil.

Nate rolled across the front lawn, digging out deep, ugly track marks in the grass. He yanked the right lever, spun the big Cat around, and headed for the front wall, just to the right of the porch.

Full throttle now. Straight on. Seat belt fastened?

————

No paper. No pencil.

Okay, okay. Uh, we had 111 on the second line. Second of twelve, that means 6 times 111 . . . Really?

He typed in 666.

ERROR. PLEASE ENTER RESET QUANTITY.

Ten seconds.

Elijah, you forgot the first decimal. "Well, picky, picky, picky!"

He typed in 666.0.

No error message.

Five seconds.

He clicked on RESET.

PROGRAM RESET. CLICK OK TO RESTART.

Don't click OK!

The numbers stopped counting down—at 2 seconds. The sirens turned off. The strobes quit flashing.

————

The blade of the bulldozer tore into the front wall of the mansion, bending, ripping, breaking. Daylight streamed in through the widening gash, and the kids began to leap and cry and cheer.

Nate backed up, took another run, and pushed the metal sheeting and framework farther aside until he had a gap wide enough for escape. He left the machine right there to hold the gap open, leaped from the seat, and gestured to the kids inside. "Come on, let's go, let's go!"

———

Leaning back in his chair, numb and exhausted, Elijah could watch the big screen on the wall above him and see the kids streaming out through that gap. He could also see his mom and dad helping each one, hugging any who needed it, and hurrying them all away from the building.

A feeble prayer escaped his lips. "Oh, God, thank you for letting me think again!" Then he looked around the incredibly complex room and shook his head. "No truth, huh? Then how did they design and build all this stuff?"

Oh-oh. He could see his mom and dad on the big screen, and he could tell they were asking about him. Elisha didn't seem to have a complete answer. She just kept pointing down, looking frantic.

"Oh, that's right. I'm the only kid still missing." He looked toward the exit door. "Guess I shouldn't keep them worrying."

epilogue

Days later, Nate sat at his computer, drafting a final report for Mr. Morgan and, via Morgan, the president.

"Most of the people arrested on that day were visitors—scholars, thinkers, academics—unfamiliar with the academy grounds and certainly not dressed for fleeing through thick forest. While not known widely by the public, these people have proven very influential in guiding the course of public education over the past fifteen to twenty years and would have had a keen interest in the experimental findings of the Knight-Moore project. Nevertheless, since none of them were directly responsible for anything that occurred at the academy, it is doubtful they can be prosecuted.

"The real perpetrators and creators of the project, known only by such dubious aliases as Bingham, Booker, Easley, Stern, and Meeks, are still at large. As I'm sure you are aware, the Knight-Moore project had the backing and protection of key people in Congress and in the Department of Education under the previous administration, and those same people can be expected to protect and hide Bingham and his friends until a more opportune time. I can only wish you God's providence in finding them.

"In the meantime, we have the children who almost perished, most of whom are safely home again, who can testify as to their experiences, as well as abundant material evidence from the academy's main control center and 'the Maze,' as my children call it. It will be an involved process, but possible, to reconstruct what the entire project was about, and to arm ourselves against letting such an agenda ever succeed."

Nate paused to admire the mountains of Montana out his office window—and to thank God for the two kids he could see out by the barn, saddling up their horses.

"Elijah is thinking and formulating more clearly than ever, thrilled with every new fact, excited just to be able to learn and know things. Elisha is composing an account of her adventure, and her first several pages reflect a depth and intensity we have never seen before. Both of them have changed in a way Bingham and his cronies hadn't counted on: Having lived in a world without truth, each has come back all the more a lover of truth and a hater of lies."

With a lump in his throat, he continued typing. "And therein lies our hope. We are a free people because we live according to what we *know* is right or wrong. If Truth is taken from us, then Right and Wrong are taken from us as well. If we don't know Right and Wrong, then we can't, we *won't* control ourselves, but will look to someone else to bring order through brute force and raw power. We will be controlled by a tyrant, and we will no longer be free—and don't count on that tyrant to be kind or merciful. He has no sense of Right and Wrong, either, and will do to us whatever he wants.

"The Knight-Moore project was an experiment to discover what would happen to people when there is no truth, to observe and record what people can do when pushed to the extreme with no ultimate moral foundation. It was an attempt by people hungry for power to find the most effective way to rob people of their freedom. The conclusion: Take away Truth, and a tyrant will rule.

"Small wonder, then, that Jesus said, 'You shall know the truth, and the truth shall make you free.' And where else can Truth, Real Truth, come from, than from God, Who is Truth by His very nature?"

Two loving arms wrapped around his shoulders. He looked up, and Sarah kissed him.

"How's it going?" she asked.

"Almost done. I'll fax it off to Morgan tonight."

Sarah looked out the window. "So, they're finally back to their horseback ride."

He smiled as they watched Elijah and Elisha climb into their saddles. "The ride they were going to take before all of this started that afternoon Morgan came."

The kids started riding, out the paddock gate and up the dirt road toward the mountain trail. The sun was bringing out all the colors of the land in summer. Elijah was singing one of his goofy songs, his head thrown back, his face to the big sky. Elisha's hair was glowing on her shoulders as she gave him her tolerant sister look.

Sarah couldn't take her eyes away. "They look so free."

Nate nodded, his arm around her. "They *are* free!"

epilogue

With a kick to their sides, the horses broke into a gallop, spiriting their young riders into the wind and the wide-open country, up a winding trail into the hills, and out of sight.